The Shake

•

Mel Nicolai

Cover photos & jacket design by Jana Perinchief

For Jana

The Shake

Mel Nicolai

Prologue

———

To kill or not to kill?

That was not the question.

If I wanted to survive, I had to kill. And I did want to survive, which changed the question from the ethical to the practical: Who and who not to kill?

But the practical question wasn't as easy to answer. For a long time, I tried to simplify the problem by telling myself that a death is a death, that they are all equally insignificant, all equally meaningless. By looking at the big picture, by viewing my actions from as great a distance as possible, I tried to neutralize my own complicity. Or at any rate, that was the idea. In practice, it didn't work all that well. No one actually lives in the big picture. In the small-picture world of particular lives, I knew my choices had consequences, and those consequences were often not to my liking.

To some extent, chance made it easier for me by delivering my victims at the end of long chains of coincidence, by paths so convoluted that the actual choices seemed inescapably random. But they weren't random. Regardless of the element of chance, I was always making choices. None of my rationalizations could erase the feeling that these choices could be right or wrong, better or worse. If I wanted to avoid killing the wrong people, I needed to understand how I was choosing. Why was I was killing one person and allowing another to live?

In the meantime, I survived.

———

I could hear and smell them as they turned the corner, a young man and a dog coming down the sidewalk in my direction. The man smelled like a broth of testosterone, sweat, tobacco, and some remarkably foul cologne. The dog smelled like a dog. From the sound of its nails scratching the cement, I knew the animal was big and not well trained. The chain rattled every time the man reined in his disobedient darling.

They were about twenty yards away when they came into view. The guy was just a kid, maybe fifteen or sixteen, wearing a baseball cap cocked at a bizarre angle, an oversized t-shirt, clownish pants with the crotch at his knees, and court shoes trailing their laces. He looked like his mommy had dressed him in preparation for some precious home video footage. The dog was a big male mastiff, bulky with muscle, as if it were on steroids. It had that nervous determination dogs have when their owners finally take them out for their daily walk.

I was sure the kid would walk by without noticing my presence. What the dog would do was anyone's guess. I waited as they drew nearer, wondering how the dice would fall. Would the dog, intended to shield its owner from a threatening world, end up being the cause of his death? People so often fell victim to their own defenses, stepping into their own traps, almost as if that had been their original intent.

I was downwind, so the dog didn't notice me until they were quite close. When it caught my scent, its body froze and its head snapped around, eyes searching the darkness as it huffed through flared nostrils. I could tell from the direction of the dog's gaze—well off to my left—that it couldn't see me. The kid had continued walking, apparently confident that when the chain's slack ran out, the dog would be pulled back into step. But the animal had other priorities. When the chain stretched taut, it just lowered itself slightly, and its master jerked to a halt.

"Justice!" the kid half shouted, yanking impatiently on the leash.

How appropriate, I thought. The dog's name was Justice. No doubt justice was what Justice was expected to dispense, to anyone or anything foolish enough to violate their private space.

"Goddamnit, dog!" the kid shouted, yanking harder on the leash, "Move your ass!"

And that's what Justice did. I made a low animal growl, just loud enough for the dog to hear. It lowered itself a couple more inches, not sure what to do, then took off like it was late for court. It shot past the kid and when it hit the end of the chain, it didn't even slow down. The kid lurched like a cartoon figure and would have bit the pavement if he hadn't let go of the leash. He yelled the dog's name again, this time more disgusted than angry, before running down the street in pursuit.

There is often something comic about a brush with death. As if, by seeing how little of life is actually under our control, we can't help laughing at the chaos of it all. Every moment teeters so delicately. We scurry about under a continuous rain of random variables, every second potentially disastrous. And all we can do is walk the dog. Our fate can be altered by the merest puff, so we bow to practicality. We inure ourselves to the chaos with our common-sense priorities. We attend to what we can process, and filter out the rest. And if we're lucky, we make it through the day. Or through the night.

•

The house I was watching was just south of Highway 50, across the freeway from the university. It belonged to Francine Arnaud, my next "donor," as I sometimes referred to people who were in line to make that singular contribution. She was twenty-eight years old, a widow, working as a clerk in a downtown law firm. I'd gathered these little facts a few weeks earlier by breaking into a psychiatrist's office and spending a couple of hours in a very comfortable, very expensive chair, reading patient files behind a very large and expensive desk. According to the good doctor, Francine had been suffering for about a year from bouts of severe depression, a condition apparently brought on by the unexpected death of her husband. On paper, she was an ideal candidate for my standard suicide scenario.

The plan for tonight was just to check out the house. There was a time when I was less cautious, less inclined to bother. But as mishap followed mishap, I finally accepted the fact that if something can go wrong, it probably will. And something can almost always go wrong.

A few years back, I was following a man I'd chosen as a suitable donor. The man had gone into his house and, on the spur of the moment, I followed him in. After taking his blood, I noticed a security camera partially hidden on a bookshelf. I searched the house thoroughly and found several others, all connected to a computer in the den. By the time I'd gotten into the computer, erased and reformatted the hard drive to make sure there wasn't any recoverable video footage, it was getting close to sunrise. I've been more careful since, accepting that precaution is the lesser inconvenience. Better safe than sunburned.

It was around 2:00 a.m. when I let myself in through Francine's unlocked back door. A good sign, I thought, the serious depressive's lack of concern for self-preservation. There was a small laundry room behind the kitchen. Dank water had collected in the bottom of the washing machine and smelled a bit like a dead rat. The door to the kitchen was closed, but the stink of garbage was palpable, even before I opened the door. The kitchen sink was full of what looked like several days' worth of dirty dishes. I went through the kitchen and the adjoining dining area into the living room. Francine Arnaud was asleep on the sofa, still in her clothes, tangled up in an old blanket. It looked like she struggled with her sleep as much as she struggled with her waking life.

I continued down the hall to the master bedroom. An undisturbed king-size bed dominated the room, giving it the look of a department store display—a space with a precisely defined function it wasn't actually serving. Everything was clean and tidy, but the tidiness, in contrast to the rest of the house, only added to the bedroom's haunted air. The dresser top was clear except for a small night lamp and a framed photograph of, I assumed, the dead husband, wearing a sheriff's uniform. He was a likable looking fellow, average build, maybe a bit on the slender side, with a pleasant, friendly smile. The kind of cop Norman Rockwell might have painted, helping an old lady cross the street.

In the closet, all of the husband's clothes were neatly hung on one side, Francine's not so neatly on the other. There was a trunk on the floor, on the husband's side. I was about to open it when I heard Francine's movements as she sat up on the sofa, then her shuffling steps as she went to the bathroom, the tinkling of her pee, the flush of the toilet, and more steps coming my way. She entered the bedroom wrapped in the old blanket. Without pulling back the covers, she crawled onto the bed, curled up in a fetal position and went back to sleep.

I could have taken her blood then, rather than wait until the following night. There wasn't any obvious advantage in waiting. It might only allow time for something unexpected to crop up and complicate matters. I wasn't as prepared as I liked to be. I hadn't brought a razor blade, so I would have to find a substitute: a kitchen knife, or something. But that was simple enough. Still, after thinking it over, I was inclined to stick to my original plan. I didn't want to be in a hurry. Human beings tend to think they don't have time to take their time. They rush through their days like their hair is on fire. It rarely occurs to them that they have it backwards. Hurrying is what they don't have time for. Haste is a form of blindness. I reminded myself of something Montaigne wrote in one of his essays: "He who does not give himself leisure to be thirsty, cannot take pleasure in drinking."

As a vampire, drinking was one of my few real pleasures, so I left the house the way I'd come.

2

———

The next evening, I was standing in the shadow of oleanders in the yard across the street from Francine's house. A light southerly breeze drifted up from the delta. The moon was a thin crescent, low on the horizon. Half a block away, a street lamp lit the intersection, but the light didn't penetrate much beyond the corner. Porch lights illuminated most of the houses, but Francine's porch was unlit. The cathode-ray flicker of her television cast its distinctive glow on her closed curtains.

I crossed the street and made my way to the back of the house. Again, the backdoor was unlocked. The kitchen was the same mess as the night before, the odor about a day more pungent. A small herd of cockroaches grazed the counter, like the contented residents of a miniature wild animal park. In the dining area separating the kitchen from the living room, the same debris littered the table, except for a space at one end that had been cleared by shoving everything toward the center. A large kitchen knife occupied the cleared space, almost glowing with suggestive intent. I couldn't help wondering if Francine had been contemplating using it on herself, a thought that was followed by one more self-serving: that what I had come there to do was somehow in accord with the young woman's own intentions.

After a century as a vampire, I still had a tendency to indulge in pointless rationalizations. When humans rationalize, they're usually trying to get away with something they might otherwise be held accountable for. They frame events in a way meant to reduce their culpability. This kind of whitewashing was completely senseless in my case, for the simple reason that I wasn't accountable to anyone. It didn't make any difference if Francine had been contemplating suicide. I didn't need permission to take her blood. Yet, I would habitually come up with ways—like calling my victims "donors"—to make them complicit in their own deaths. As if I needed to convince myself that I was simply acting as a surrogate in a progression of inevitable events over which I had no control.

It wasn't a very clever evasion, and in the end only highlighted the fact that I didn't understand my own choices. It wouldn't have been a problem, except that I wanted there to be a distinction. I wanted life and death to be somehow deserved. And I wanted there to be a way to decide who deserved which. I felt there should be a way to make the distinction; a way that wasn't completely arbitrary. But I didn't know how to do that. So I was reduced to rationalizing my choices. At best, I chose my victims on the basis of practical concerns over my own safety, killing people whose circumstances offered me a way to cover my tracks.

I could have circumvented the whole issue by meeting my dietary requirements with non-human blood. I'd tried more than once. Relying on non-human sources offered definite logistical advantages, but in the long run it just didn't work. A few months of nothing but cow and horse blood, and I would begin to feel a subtle and debilitating loss of vigor, as if my metabolism were slowing down in some protective response to malnutrition. It wasn't life-threatening. I suspect I could have survived indefinitely on non-human blood. But it would have been an impoverished existence. I could live on animal blood, but to live well I needed the sapiens vintage.

Unfortunately, dead people whose bodies have been drained of blood attract a lot of attention. If I wanted to stay in one location for any length of time, I couldn't litter the neighborhood with dehydrated corpses. Sooner or later, I'd become suspect, and at that point, I'd have no real choice but to relocate. I liked where I was living. I liked being settled, having a fixed abode. So I had to find ways of feeding regularly that minimized the risks.

The question was, who to target? It made sense, I thought, to look for people who had already been marginalized by society, people about whom I could rely on a maximum level of indifference from the authorities. My first thought was to target criminals. The police might be relieved, even entertained, by the terminal misfortunes of my victims. This idea wasn't completely without merit, but there was a definite drawback to harvesting the criminal contingent: they were people whose activities were already integrated into the vast intersecting networks of law enforcement. More than an occasional odd death would soon set off alarms. In short, the criminals were as much a part of the system as were the police. Which made them an impractical choice as a dietary staple.

Then it occurred to me that there was a group of people who were made to order. Death among them was never really unexpected. And once dead, they were quickly and efficiently consigned to the anonymity of statistics. Bureaucratic indifference would summarily record their departures and just as summarily forget them. As luck would have it, such people were an abundant commodity. In fact, they comprised a significant percentage of the human population. They fell under a spectrum of medical and psychiatric classifications, but what they all had in common was depression. Most of them had at least thought about suicide, and many had made half-hearted attempts. When they succeeded, the police treated their deaths as a formality, filed their reports and trudged back to their case loads. Perfect, really. I could expedite their desire to end it all, and it would be exactly what everyone half expected.

Still, as abundant as the depressed were, I couldn't harvest them like fruit from an abandoned orchard. In a sense, they had their own niche in the human ecology. Exploiting them for their blood required a significant amount of resource management. They would remain a viable staple only so long as I didn't kill too many. On the bright side, the resource management gave me something to do with my time, dreaming up ways to cull the herd without attracting the law, planning all the details. The down side was that each meal required a lot of work. It wasn't something I could do more than a couple of times a month. I still needed a source of human blood that I could take quickly, without much planning or preparation, and walk away unthreatened.

I suppose I was a little slow in coming up with a solution, but when it finally dawned on me, I realized immediately I had a made-to-order supply of human blood pretty much on tap. Every year in the U.S., over 40,000 people die in traffic accidents. That's well over one hundred a day. These deaths are so routine that they pass unquestioned. There may be inquiries made for the purpose of establishing insurance liabilities, and in some cases, to determine if any criminal misconduct was to blame. But the deaths themselves are explained by their occurrence: death by car crash. If a car goes off the road and hits a tree, there is very little chance that the accident will be attributed to the mischief of a vampire.

All I needed was a dark night, a winding road, perhaps some rain or fog. Add to that the nearly universal tendency of humans to press their luck by driving as fast as they think they can get away with; all these combined to create an ideal scenario for a thirsty vampire. Not that I could just wait by the side of the road, hoping someone would oblige me by driving into a tree. I had to encourage drivers to make the necessary course adjustments.

I would wait along a winding road for a lone driver and walk casually in front of their oncoming car. The driver would hit the brakes, swerve, maybe close his eyes and hope for the best. For my part, all I had to do was jump a few feet into the air and let the car pass under me. Or if I wasn't in the mood for gymnastics, I could snatch someone's pet—a medium-sized dog was just right for the job—and wait for the lone car. As it approached, I'd simply throw the dog against the car's windshield. Very few people can keep their cool in a situation like that. When everything went as planned, the car would go off the road. If the driver was lucky not to be hurt, he'd have a real roller coaster ride and a good story to tell, and I would let him live to tell his tale. Those that weren't so lucky were my supper.

In one respect, it was a game of random selection. I had no control over who might drive by on any given night. But it really wasn't random. I was still deciding which of the many passing cars I would step in front of. I even managed to rationalize this. I told myself that, by people's own standards, a full and successful life was best measured by one's possessions. People with all the expensive toys had already enjoyed their fair share of life. So I'd let the ten-year-old pickups and economy sedans pass, telling myself it was more equitable to terminate the driver of a Mercedes or a BMW. This kind of pseudo-reasoning was completely unconvincing, but with my need for blood and no way to make an objective choice of who to kill, I was reduced to this kind of weak-minded rationalization. Like people, I was usually ready to abandon my critical faculties whenever they failed to serve my self-interest.

At any rate, between the staged suicides, the car accidents, and the lucky chance opportunities that occasionally presented themselves, I was able to feed on human blood at least three or four times a month. The rest of the time, drawing blood from horses and cattle provided an abundant supply of adequate nourishment to tide me over between real meals. This methodical moderation, this submission to a program of planned management, was an acceptable price to pay for a permanent residence. The stability, I told myself, made up for the lack of adventure. I would eventually get tired of it. Either that, or one of life's little surprises would bring it all crashing down. But in the meantime...

In the living room, the TV was on, but the sound was turned all the way down. Like the night before, Francine was asleep on the sofa. She was lying on her left side, her back to the TV, with the same old blanket pulled up around her shoulders. I knelt beside her and listened to her breathing. There was a slight wheeze when she inhaled. When she exhaled, her breath smelled surprisingly fresh, as if the vitality of her body had resisted the decline of her spirit.

I lifted the blanket away from her shoulders. She was still dressed in her work clothes. The motion of the blanket released the scent of her body, unmasked by perfume. Even after a century separating me from my human past, certain sensations, particularly odors, still occasionally ambushed me, transporting me back to that other life. The sweat of this young woman's body was momentarily transfixing. A hundred years ago, I would have been entranced by it. But those were only memories. However precise they might be, they were drained of emotional content, irrelevant to my current concerns.

Gently, I placed my left hand at the base of her neck, and with my right hand simultaneously pinched her nose closed and covered her mouth. There was a moment of sleepy resistance, then her eyes sprang open. When I turned her head, rolling her onto her back so she could more comfortably see me, her eyes flared even wider with panic. She tried to inhale, but only created a vacuum pulling against the palm of my hand.

People don't always behave predictably in a situation like this. Some are fighters and will take the struggle to the bitter end. There was a time when I judged the fighters to be worthy of higher regard. They didn't just give up after a brief, token struggle. I couldn't understand someone who wouldn't fight for their own life; who acted as if resisting death were no more than a formality that had to be gotten through, and the sooner the better. But I no longer felt that way. I knew from experience that fighting could be a form of acquiescence, and what might first appear as passivity could in reality be the most stubborn resistance, a desperate tactic driven by a fierce determination to prevail. The latter was fairly common among women. Smaller and physically weaker, women have had to find more subtle ways to turn the tide in their favor.

Francine, however, neither fought nor feigned. I wondered

if her passivity was a symptom of her depression. Maybe she had already thrown in her cards and was glad to let unconsciousness insulate her from the only thing she now expected from life: more pain. Whatever the reason, she fainted straightaway. When her body went slack, I removed my hand from her face. She inhaled once quickly, then her breathing steadied. I lifted the blanket and draped it over the back of the sofa, then picked her up and carried her into the master bedroom.

I laid her on the bed and undressed her. She had a lovely body. Her skin was very pale, almost white, with small breasts and small, pink nipples. There was a tattoo of a ladybug on a leaf on the left side of her abdomen, just above her pubic hair. An inch-long scar paralleled her left kneecap. Her feet were small, the toes slender and straight, as if they had never been tortured by stylish shoes. They smelled of sweat and leather.

I picked her up again and carried her into the bathroom, laying her gently in the tub. I expected her to wake up when her bare skin made contact with the cold porcelain, but she didn't. I turned on the water, adjusting it to a comfortable warmth, and watched as the water line slowly edged its way up her torso. When the tub was about two thirds full, I shut off the faucets.

There was nothing left to do except finish what I had come for. Yet, I hesitated. It wasn't the woman's naked body that gave me pause, but my own lack of reaction to her body. I should have been used to it, but it still intrigued me that the human female, though no different in form than a female vampire, did not arouse in me the slightest sexual desire. The woman before me was undeniably beautiful. I could appreciate her beauty, but I felt no desire to possess her physically. I was as sexually

15

indifferent to her as I would have been to the beauty of a flower or to some finely crafted *objet d'art*.

I had come to think of this absence of feeling as a symptom of the distance separating me from humans; a distance that time had steadily increased. But lately I'd begun to wonder if I might not have it all wrong. Maybe I wasn't being honest with myself. Maybe my detachment was a way of protecting myself, not from the gap separating me from humans, but from the narrowness of that gap. As the years passed, I had told myself I was moving farther and farther away from humanity. I believed this growing separation was inevitable, a result of the physical conditions of my existence. I lived far longer than humans. I was not vulnerable to human diseases. My senses were far keener and my physical prowess beyond comparison. And on top of all that, I drank human blood, which reduced the human population to a food supply.

But at the same time, as the essential differences between human and vampire became more inescapable, I was gradually growing more conscious of an equally inescapable similarity; a similarity that would never go away. We, vampires and humans, both tell ourselves stories about ourselves, and about each other. I could not evade the fact that this was a part of me that was fundamentally and permanently human. This process of story telling was the very tool I used to understand those things that supposedly distanced and distinguished me from people. In other words, the explanations I gave myself of how different I was were themselves an ineradicable mark of sameness.

I had a knack for dawdling over this sort of speculation, but I had to cut it short. There were more immediate concerns. Taking Francine's left hand, I held her arm above the water's surface and, with the razor blade I had brought along for the purpose, made a deep incision along the length of the vein in her wrist. There was a brief pause before blood began to pulse out of the cut. I leaned over and placed my lips around the opening, taking what I had come for. When she was close to death, I lowered her arm into the water.

Only a couple more things to do, to encourage the police to handle her death as a routine suicide. I cleaned my prints off the razor blade, then carefully pressed the thumb and forefinger of her right hand several times onto the blade, making sure it was covered with her prints, then dropped it into the bath. I had drunk most of her blood, so there wasn't enough in the bath water to indicate that she'd bled to death. To fix that, I carefully loosened the drain plug so that the water would slowly drain out. By the time someone discovered her body, the tub would be empty and dry. It would look like her blood had simply gone down the drain along with the water.

I went back to the bedroom and folded her clothes, stacking them neatly on the bed. Noticing the photo of her husband on the dresser, I thought it would be a nice touch, in the absence of a suicide note, to use the photo as a poignant gesture of farewell, and moved it to the bed next to her folded clothes. Then I remembered the trunk in the closet. The night before, I'd been about to open it when Francine had gotten up from the sofa and come into the bedroom. I didn't have any particular reason to be interested in the trunk's contents, beyond a certain fascination with people's mementos. More often than not, what I found curious about the artifacts humans chose to invest with sentimental value was their dreary uniformity, but that never seemed to curtail my curiousity.

17

It was early and I didn't have anything else to do, so I turned on the closet light and slid the trunk out from under the hanging clothes. The contents were about what I'd expected, the usual junk stacked in sedimentary layers: a few old toys and memorabilia from childhood, a little league uniform, baseball glove, a box of photos, high school yearbooks, college diploma, and so on. Another little treasure chest of mediocrity. These artifacts were hardly evidence of a unique life. But then, maybe people just needed to remind themselves that they were normal. This guy's name was Dean, and if the memorabilia could be trusted, he was pretty normal.

There was, however, one item of interest: a manila folder wedged in the back with the word "LIES" printed in block letters on the front. The envelope contained a collection of newspaper clippings and other documents relating to Dean Arnaud's death. I was curious about what "LIES" referred to, so I sat down on the floor of the closet and began to read.

The newspaper clippings chronicled Dean's unsolved murder, along with the scandal of an alleged connection to drug trafficking. His body had been found by a maid in a Vacaville motel. Someone had put a single small-caliber bullet in the back of Dean's head. There were traces of cocaine in the room, both on the nightstand and in the bathroom, and the coroner's report showed cocaine in Dean's blood. The whole business was apparently an embarrassment for the Sheriff's Department. Arnaud was not officially involved in any drug-related cases and was off duty at the time of his death. The sheriff's investigation was inconclusive. No arrests were ever made.

Along with the newspaper clippings were copies of several letters Francine had written to various officials in local and state law enforcement, as well as to California's attorney general and the governor's office. These were emotional pleas to find her husband's murderer and clear his name. She was positive Dean had not been involved in any form of illegal activity. It was inconceivable, to her at least, that he was either selling or using drugs.

There were responses to some of these letters; all sympathetic and sincere expressions of bureaucratic buck-passing and indifference. In the absence of new evidence, everything that could be done was being done. The case was still open, but due to limited resources and case loads, blah blah blah. There was also a business card for Hamilton Investigations, LLC. The card was paper clipped together with two receipts for services rendered and a photograph cut out of the newspaper.

That was when things started to get more interesting. The face of the man in the photo was familiar, but it took a second to register. His name was Ron Richardson, a local real estate tycoon and building contractor. By all outward appearances, Ron was a respected member of the community, an active supporter of numerous cultural and charitable foundations, a family man with two happily married daughters, and a devout, though sadly divorced, Catholic. Outward appearances aside, he was also a major player in northern California's illegal drug trade.

Ever since the drug business really started to take off, back in the 60s, traffickers had been a particular interest of mine. I kept an eye on the people who ran these organizations and was in fact indebted to them. I owed a large part of my financial independence to the fact that, operating as they do in an illegal and magnificently lucrative business, they often have very large sums of cash in their possession. Snatching a slice of their pie now and then was an easy way to fatten my bank account.

Richardson had been on my watch list for a couple of years. I'd been playing with the idea of coercing him into some kind of relationship that would allow me to forego the inconvenience of having to steal his money. There were basically two ways I could have gone about this. The less appealing would have been to provide him with some kind of service. I wasn't too keen on this approach. It went against my general policy of avoiding complicated business arrangements with humans. The other approach was more to my liking: extort the money by scaring him senseless.

Ron seemed to be fairly typical of people in the higher echelons of the drug business. Barbarians, basically, these were people whose arrogance provided them with all the justification they needed to remain indifferent to the damage and suffering their greed inflicted on their fellow humans. In that sense, I suppose he wasn't much different from your typical businessman. Typically, too, he put considerable effort into promoting his public image. Considering the scope of his illegal activities, quiet anonymity would have made more sense. But Richardson wasn't the quiet type. His vanity required him to be in the limelight. I was curious how someone like him could manage to keep his public persona so pristine. I didn't know of any negative publicity suggesting that the police were aware of his drug trafficking activities. This could have meant he was both smarter and more cautious than most. But more likely it meant that he was paying off all the right people.

Finding Richardson's photo in Francine's trunk was an unexpected coincidence, but little more than that. I probably would have dropped the matter had it not been for one other little detail. In the same block letters used on the envelope, Francine had printed the word "BLOODSUCKER" on the back of Richardson's photo. I sat for a minute contemplating this word, "BLOODSUCKER." It wasn't a term I preferred to use in reference to those of my kind. In Richardson's case the intent was no doubt figurative. The blood Richardson sucked from his victims was in the form of dollars. But it was one of those little blips on the radar that sometimes teased my sense of synchronicity.

Maybe Francine had discovered some reason to doubt Richardson's public image. Maybe she even had reason to think Richardson was involved in her husband's death. From a purely practical standpoint, if Richardson was mixed up in Dean's murder, I might be able to use the threat of exposure to leverage money out of him. Of course, I didn't need that kind of leverage. I was quite capable of applying my own. Either way, I thought it might be worth looking into. If I could uncover something that might make it easier to extort money from Richardson, fine. If not, it wouldn't matter. I could fall back on my own distinctive methods of coercion.

I put everything back in the trunk, then returned to the bathroom for a final check on Francine. The water in the tub had already drained down several inches. Perfect. I left by the back door, locking it on the way out so the police would be less likely to suspect she'd had visitors.

3

Any traumatic event can leave one feeling like his life has been split in two, divided into a before and after. War often does this to men who have survived combat. Natural disasters or a near-fatal illness can have the same effect. But no matter how traumatic an event might be, it will not break the underlying continuity of being human. Only death does that. Or becoming a vampire.

Being turned severed me from my human past. The split was not total—remnants have survived from my former existence—but the underlying continuity was cut. The first forty years of my life provided the raw material for what I was to become, but the change was so nearly total that the human part of my life seemed to be stripped of significance. Becoming a vampire was a corner around which, once turned, I could not look back. I don't mean that I lost all memory of my human past. I remembered it well enough. But I couldn't look back to my former life and hope to find answers about the present, about what I had become. For all practical purposes, the only life that meant anything to me began in 1908.

I was on leave at the time from a small private college in New York where, ironically, I taught humanities. My wife, Rose, and I had decided to spend a few months in Sicily and had rented a small cottage in Messina. Rose was an amateur archaeologist and was interested in the history of Sicily. I had been looking forward to the quiet and relative solitude to work on a paper I'd been writing. Like most academics, I suppose I had a rather inflated opinion of the importance of my own ideas. I took it for granted that my status as a professional gave me an authority that extended beyond the confines of my specific discipline. In short, I was a moderately pompous ass, but with a gift for gab and a quirky personality that made me popular in the lecture hall.

Our first night in Messina, my wife and I were sleeping, each in one of the bedroom's two single beds. Shortly after 5:00 a.m., something that couldn't happen happened. Something monstrous entered our room, sank its teeth into my wife's neck, and sucked her life away.

At the time, I would have denied the very possibility that an extravagant creature from folk tales actually walked the earth the same as I did. My entire adult life, as I saw it, had been devoted to freeing myself from the various fallacies and superstitions of the past. A vampire was a scientific impossibility. Rationality banned the idea from consideration, and as so often happens in this life, reality bit back.

Rose was a petite woman. Her blood failed to satisfy the vampire's thirst. When her heart stopped, it was my turn. I remember having one of those dreams in which some disturbing element of the surroundings is integrated into the details of the dream. I dreamed of a weight pinning my body to the bed, a vague irritation on my neck, a swirling descent. Had nature not intervened, those dreamed sensations would have been the final illusions of my life.

At 5:20 a.m., seconds after the vampire had bitten into my neck, the city of Messina was struck by a devastating earthquake. Like most of the buildings of Sicily, our cottage was made of stone. The initial shock collapsed the wall next to my bed, along with the roof it was supporting. I woke wide-eyed just as the whole thing came crumbling down on top of me. I felt the stones hit, but instead of crushing me, there was only the sudden impact of great weight cushioned by something that had absorbed most of the blow. Something on top of me had shielded me from injury. I heard a low, animal-like growl, half pain, half fury, then whatever it was coughed in a single convulsive spasm and a gush of blood sprayed my face. That spray of blood was the baptism of my new life.

As far as I could tell, I wasn't injured, but I couldn't move under the weight of the rubble. There was an intermittent stench every time the thing on top of me exhaled. It was making me nauseous, but I couldn't turn my face enough to avoid it. Then I remembered Rose. In a horror of panic, I tried to free myself, kicking and twisting with all my strength. I managed to scrape the skin off my shins and elbows, but didn't accomplish anything else. I called her name several times, but there was no answer. The night was silent except for the wheezing breath of my companion and the throbbing of my own pulse in my ears. I tried again to free myself, but it was pointless. The end had come. I resigned myself to the inevitable and soon lost consciousness.

I don't know how long I was out. Pain eventually woke me up. My neck was on fire and I was experiencing an unbearable agitation, like electric heat that seemed to be radiating from every cell of my body. Waves of some nauseating energy swept through me, and I hurt, everywhere. The pain was beyond anything I had ever experienced. My entire body seemed to be generating it, each wave growing more intense, until the agony made me long for death.

Again, mercifully, I passed out.

The next time I woke up, everything had changed. Of course, at the time I had no inkling of what had happened to me. The existence of vampires was not something I would have been willing to entertain. And the fact that they didn't exist would only make it that much harder to adjust to the awkward fact that I had become one. As if life wasn't hard enough without turning into a mythical beast.

Rescue operations after the earthquake were slow and disorganized, primarily due to the extent of destruction, which was almost total, and the extraordinarily high number of casualties. When I regained consciousness, I realized the darkness was no longer total, though only the faintest indirect light penetrated the rubble. As far as I could determine, we, myself and the thing on top of me, were trapped in a space no larger than our bodies. I knew my companion was still alive because I could hear and feel him breathing. I could also still smell his breath, which had become both more intense and, curiously, less revolting.

The following day was a long one. I don't know how many times I passed in and out of consciousness. Each time I woke up, I seemed to be suffering less physically, and for reasons I didn't understand, I also seemed to be less concerned about the predicament I was in. Nothing external had changed. I was still trapped and I had no reason to think I would be rescued. The old me, the humanities teacher, would have found his impending death somewhat distressing. Like most people, the old me was reasonably adept at feeling sorry for himself. But as the hours slowly passed, the familiar moods of despair and self-pity became increasingly less engaging.

In fact, I felt calmer and more detached than I could remember ever feeling. There I was, trapped under a heap of stone, my wife's dead body no doubt only a few feet away. I was sharing what would most likely be my grave with a mysterious and malodorous companion, silent except for his snoring. And I didn't seem to have a care in the world. When I thought about it, the only thing I felt was an unusual sense of strength. I felt so strong, I was sure I could now push my way out of the rubble.

Lying on my back, I had almost no freedom of movement. I could raise my left knee a few inches, but not my right. I could manage some lateral movement with both arms, but I couldn't raise my torso enough to get any leverage. I was exploring these possibilities when my companion spoke.

"Not yet," he said, calmly. "The sun is still up."

Under different circumstances, that might have scared me to death.

"Confusing, isn't it?" the voice added, with dreamy tranquility.

I was reluctant to say anything. It was as if by speaking I would enter into some form of complicity, and I wasn't sure I wanted to do that.

"Anyway, it's too risky to move the stones by yourself," the voice continued, with calm authority. "We'll do it together, later, when it's dark outside. In the meantime, you should rest."

His name, I would soon learn, was Calvin. At the time, some part of me already suspected he had something to do with my wife's death. That part of me wanted to be enraged by the injustice. I couldn't understand why another part of me was pushing that rage into the background, forcing my feelings to recede. It was as if years had passed since her death, instead of only hours. I thought it might be due to the ambiguity of the situation; the mixing up of the injustice of her murder with the moral neutrality of a natural catastrophe. But this thought, too, was rejected by some unfamiliar part of me. It was as if this unfamiliar part knew very clearly what had happened, and it wasn't letting me indulge in my familiar moods.

It was, indeed, confusing. It was as if the very core of my personal identity was being erased by something cold and inhuman. And most confusing of all was that I didn't seem to be particularly bothered by it. At any rate, not bothered enough to stop myself from drifting back into sleep. Some hours must have passed before his voice woke me again.

"What do you say? Shall we stretch our legs?"

The question made me laugh. It was as if extricating ourselves from the rubble wouldn't be any more difficult than stepping out to the porch for a smoke. And as it turned out, it wasn't. Once free, I immediately became preoccupied with the range and intensity of my senses. At first, I thought this might be the experience of heightened awareness one hears people speak of after a brush with death; the feeling of an intensification of life that, I assumed, would soon pass. There were a couple of problems with that explanation, though. I was as emotionally detached as I had ever been in my life. And things were not returning to normal.

The moon was just a thin crescent, yet by its light I could see clearly, several paces away, a tiny beetle crawling along the shadowed edge of a rock. Fifty paces away, amid the city's fresh ruins, I could see the glittering eyes of rats. I could hear their claws scratching on stone. All around me, I could smell the violent death hidden under the collapsed buildings. And somewhere in the distance I could hear the faint muffled crying of a child.

Calvin sat on a large slab of fallen wall, swinging his dangling feet like a dreamy young girl gazing at the moon. It struck me suddenly that, of all the horror surrounding me, he was the only thing that unnerved me. He was obviously indifferent to the panorama of destruction. And I knew he had been injured. My hair, neck and shoulders were still caked with his dried blood. But in less than a single day, he had miraculously recovered and seemed to be in perfect health.

I had a lot of questions and Calvin seemed to offer the best chance of getting answers, but I hadn't even opened my mouth when he jumped down from his perch and dusted himself off.

"Well then," he said, as if something had been resolved, "I'll be on my way."

"On your way?" I asked, dumbfounded.

Calvin stopped and looked at me with the expression of a man momentarily vexed by the discovery of some trivial annoyance, like a stubborn piece of lint stuck to his jacket. "Is there something on your mind?" he asked, not the slightest suggestion in his voice that he was interested in an answer.

I wanted to get angry, but I was too confused by my own inability to call up the familiar emotions. "Yes," I said, more calmly than I'd anticipated, "there is something on my mind. To begin with, what the hell happened?"

Calvin briefly considered my question. "It wasn't my intention to turn you. But it's done now and undoing it would be unpleasant for you and more effort than it's worth for me. I realize it's disorienting, but you'll get over it. The thirst will educate you. And frankly, nothing else matters."

I had no idea what he was talking about. "The thirst?" I asked.

Calvin paused, deliberating over a response, then apparently changed his mind. "I'm sorry," he said, turning to go, "but I don't have much time, or much interest in this sort of thing."

I watched him walk away, perplexed by my own willingness to accept the situation at face value. About thirty yards away, Calvin stopped and turned. "You'll need to find a dark and private place. Before dawn."

•

I had a rough time those first few weeks. I was like a container filled with the memories of a human being, but they were memories in which I could no longer recognize myself. And the container was leaking. The human being was dripping away, steadily replaced by something deeply unfamiliar. As the human part of me faded, I found myself clinging to it ever more desperately. I would find myself drawn to people, only to be repelled, as if what I thought were men and women turned out to be only cardboard cutouts. Cardboard cutouts, that is, filled with blood.

When I finally realized it was blood that was drawing me to people, I was sure I was doomed, sure I would never be able to take what my body was telling me it needed. And when, after so short a time, I proved myself wrong, it was only to find myself strangely and powerfully repulsed by the act of feeding on humans. Not because of moral considerations, but rather, as a result of a straightforward physical response. Taking someone's blood made me feel like I had been reduced to blind, instinctual drives. I felt like an insect that had sucked the protoplasm out of its prey, leaving behind an empty husk. That human husk really gave me the creeps.

I tried for a while to survive on animal blood. Ironically, it was something lingering from my human past that made taking the blood of animals so distasteful. Even as a child, I'd had a violent aversion to the feeling of hair in my mouth. In my adult life, this aversion had been the occasion for some delicate negotiations. My wife, for instance, had initially reacted skeptically to my request that she shave her pubic hair. She had some trouble getting past her suspicion that I was under the sway of some prepubescent perversion. As a vampire, the hair problem took on a new and, while it lasted, daunting dimension. Mammals—dogs, horses, cows—are all covered with hair. As absurd as it sounds, the choice between reducing a human to a dehydrated husk or biting into the hairy hide of an animal wasn't an easy one. Not at first, anyway. But the dilemma didn't last long. It was just another piece of human baggage that, once dropped, I couldn't quite figure out what the fuss had been about.

The hair problem was typical of many of the adjustments I had to make in my new life. They weren't always easy, or without consequence, but for the most part, they were rather trivial. Resolving them was usually just a matter of replacing an old habit with a new one. Other problems proved to be more intractable, rooted as they were in a fundamental paradox.

Once turned, it was only natural that my new powers

would occupy my attention. Discovering what it meant to be a vampire plunged me into a near-constant state of astonishment. But as the novelty wore off, a part of me that had not changed gradually insinuated itself. This stubbornly human part of me had to do with the act of thinking. Not a matter of beliefs and opinions, nor of personality, it was deeper than that. I had learned to think, speak and communicate as a human being, in a human language. As a vampire, my thought processes might differ somewhat from those of humans, but only insofar as the contingencies of my life forced incidental modifications upon those still-human processes. The fact that I drank human blood, for instance, forced me to think differently about the value of human life. I might tell myself that drinking human blood was analogous to a human eating a chicken sandwich. People reduce the living chicken to broiled meat, erasing any consideration of status that might be given to the chicken. A comparable process compels a vampire to erase considerations of status that might otherwise be given to humans. But the entire constellation of arguments, reasons, judgments, and justifications was itself unmistakably human. The uncomfortable truth was that my ties to humanity were deeply and inescapably paradoxical.

4

———

Before squeezing a little monetary juice out of Ron Richardson, I was hoping to find a new driver. I appreciated the utility of a car, but I had never been particularly fond of driving. I put up with it for a few years, back in the forties, but eventually gave it up in favor of a chauffeur. Hiring a human introduced complications into my life, but there were practical advantages, too. Chief among them being that a driver could run errands for me during daylight hours.

I had lost my previous driver a couple of months back. White, as he liked to be called for some reason I never understood, since it wasn't his name, had been pulled over for speeding. I wasn't with him at the time, which was no doubt fortunate for all concerned. Apparently he had shown a lack of respect sufficient to warrant a trip to the police station. Once there, his behavior continued to deteriorate, and he ended up behind bars. He then took another step down the ladder of respectability when the police opened the trunk of his car—the car I had provided—and found a half dozen illegal automatic weapons.

The whole business was far less sinister than it was made out to be. White may have been an obnoxious little shit, but he was essentially harmless. The guns weren't his. He was transporting them for someone else. He refused, initially, to rat out the owner of the weapons, adopting a hard-ass "I'm no snitch" posture that he'd probably picked up from the movies. His resolve lasted for an hour or so before he caved in and told the police who owned the guns. White got off easy with a suspended sentence and probation. None of it would have mattered much to me if the presiding judge had not also revoked his driver's license.

As it was, I hadn't been very satisfied with White's job performance, and was thinking about getting rid of him, anyway. He definitely had not been my best-ever choice for a driver. As is so often the case with humans, White was full of unpleasant surprises. He could project a veneer of modest competence, but it was just a smoke screen for the trash heap of dysfunction underneath. Losing his driver's license settled the matter of his employment, leaving one little loose end to tie up. I was never very comfortable with firing an employee. Once out of my employ, once the money stopped flowing, they seemed to forget the rules, or they would make the mistake of thinking that the rules no longer applied. It was more prudent for me to terminate them, literally, even though I knew that feeding on someone with whom I had frequent contact could involve additional risk. In White's case, I was spared both the inconvenience and the risk. Apparently the owner of the illegal guns was as unhappy with White as I had been. The day after his release from custody, White was found dead from multiple gunshot wounds.

Which left me without a driver. Unfortunately, a good driver wasn't easy to find. I couldn't just put an ad in the newspaper: "Vampire seeks chauffeur. Call for midnight interview." All I could do was keep my eye out for possible candidates. This might take a long time, and often did, but there wasn't any practical alternative. On this particular occasion, I thought I might have gotten lucky. A few days prior to my

33

rendezvous with Francine, I'd spotted someone I thought might fill the bill. She worked in a place called the Triple Tavern on West Capital Avenue. A fairly sad place, as they go, it catered to dedicated local drunks, truckers, and prostitutes. Apparently, she also turned tricks in one of the many motels along the avenue that did business by the hour.

That was how she first caught my attention. It was about 2:00 a.m. and I was taking a little stroll, not particularly hungry because I had gorged myself the previous night on a young Arabian mare pastured in Fair Oaks. I was walking past a motel parking lot, when the door to one of the rooms flew open and a young woman lunged out of the brightly lit interior into the parking lot's semidarkness. She was wearing panties and high heels, carrying the rest of her clothes bunched under one arm, and she was clearly pissed about something. Once outside, she balanced herself against a parked car with her free hand, bent over and spit blood on the pavement.

When she leaned on the car, she set off the alarm. These devices were as irritating to her as they were to me. Screaming "Fuck," she spun around and slammed her fist onto the hood of the car. This seemed to help her focus and she began to dress herself. She had just gotten her jeans on when a man stepped into the motel room's open doorway. Apparently the reason for her hasty exit, he was holding the side of his head and there was a lot blood running down his face and onto his chest. He seemed more confused than angry. He took a step toward the woman, but then changed his mind and sat down on the doorstep. He was a big guy. He looked like he was in his early forties, well over six feet tall, around two-fifty. It took some spunk for a woman to lay into a guy like that.

34

As the guy sat down, the door to the adjoining room opened. An older man in a bathrobe stood there for a moment, assessing the scene, then pointed his electronic gizmo at the car. The alarm stopped screeching, he shook his head sadly and closed the door.

By then the woman had the rest of her clothes on. She turned toward the guy still sitting there bleeding, took two quick steps toward him and spat. "Asshole!" she hissed, then turned and stalked out of the parking lot.

I watched her cross the street to the Triple Tavern parking lot where she got into an older model Honda Civic, and drove away. I liked the looks of her. Spirited, with a temper, but rather precise in her actions. A woman capable of making compromises in the name of survival, but with lines she wouldn't cross. Not inclined to take a lot of shit, but with the good judgment to walk away when the situation called for it. Punctuating her exit by spitting in the guy's face added a certain charm, as well.

This had taken place on a Thursday night. I confirmed the following evening that she worked at the tavern where she had parked her car the night before, and decided to pay a visit. I wore my usual black tennis shoes, jeans, and a black T-shirt. As usual, I looked like some kind of pseudo-beatnik, nerd-gothic wannabe, so I added a dark gray sport coat to give myself a slightly more moneyed appearance.

It was a little after 11:00 p.m. There were seven cars in the parking lot, including the woman's Honda. Including the woman, there were seven people in the tavern. She was behind the bar. An older man, probably in his sixties, was sitting at a corner table, adding up receipts on a pocket calculator. The expression on his thin, deeply lined face suggested a habitual dissatisfaction with what the calculator was telling him. Five customers, four men and a woman, occupied seats at the bar and tables, chosen as if to maximize the space between themselves. Three of the men were in their fifties or sixties, the other one looked barely old enough to drink. The only female patron looked to be about forty, but she might have been younger. It was hard to tell. Alcohol is as unkind to the body as a desert wind.

The room was dark, the smell of booze and tobacco riding on a base-odor of moldy carpet. A jukebox along the back wall was emitting something country-like, though at a mercifully low volume. Competing with the jukebox, a TV behind the bar aired the news. It was hard to tell if anyone was paying attention to either.

Even when I was human, I wasn't much of a drinker. I'd have a glass of beer occasionally, or wine with dinner, but I never understood the appeal of alcohol. It was probably just a matter of body chemistry. Some people like it, some don't. My updated vampire metabolism left me completely indifferent to it. I wasn't sure if I could actually get drunk, even if I were to try, which I never had.

An aversion to alcohol might make spending time in a bar somewhat awkward, if alcohol was the issue. But, like most everything else, the real issue was money. Alcohol was just a way to move it out of one person's pocket and into someone else's. As long as I was parting with some of mine, no one was likely to object to my distaste for the liquid. I chose a stool at the unpopulated end of the bar. The woman came over immediately and asked me what I wanted. I ordered a Scotch. When she came back with the drink, I gave her a ten and told her to keep the change.

She looked surprised. "That drink's only five bucks," she said, making sure I really wanted to tip her the other five.

"No doubt worth every penny," I said.

She shrugged, went to the cash register, put the ten in, took out a five, folded it neatly and slipped it into her jeans pocket. I took my drink and moved to an empty booth. I didn't have any particular plan in mind. I thought I would just sit for a while and observe. Not that there was much to see. After a few minutes, one guy got up and fed some change into the jukebox. The guy on the bar stool provided occasional commentary on the TV news, consisting of either "Shit!" or "More shit!" I had to admit, I was in complete agreement, especially with the "More shit!" The lone female customer held up her empty glass indicating the need for a refill. When the drink arrived, I heard her say, "Thanks, Karla," and thereby learned the barkeep's name.

After about half an hour, Karla approached my booth. She saw I hadn't touched my drink. "Something wrong with the Scotch, honey?" she asked.

"I'm sure it's fine," I said. "I'm just waiting for the mood to strike."

She looked at her watch. "We close in about two and half hours."

"Sardonic wit," I said. Then added, curious to see how she would react, "And a pierced nipple."

Anger flashed in her eyes. "What the fuck do you know about my nipples?" she demanded, her fists on her hips.

"I saw you the other night at the motel across the street. In the parking lot, remember? With the charming gentleman leaking blood."

The wheels were turning. She wasn't happy with my nose in her private affairs. But at the same time, she was curious.

"You're not the guy with the car alarm, are you?"

"No, I just happened to be passing by."

"And thought you'd stop and watch the show?"

"Something like that," I admitted.

Her annoyance seemed to pass. "So, what's it to you, anyway?" she asked.

"What'd you hit him with?"

"An ashtray. The stupid fucker backhanded me."

There was a cut on her lower lip which was still slightly swollen. I touched my own lip, indicating her injury. She responded by bringing her hand up and lightly touching the swollen area. "You want anything else?" she asked, apparently finished with the conversation.

"As a matter of fact, there is something else. I'd like to talk to you when you have a few minutes."

"I'll bet you would," she said, as if she now had me figured out. "That little show last night turn you on?"

She was a straightforward girl. There was no reason not to be straightforward in return. "It is a business matter," I said, "but not that kind of business. Something you might find to your liking. Just chat with me for a few minutes when you have a break. If you're not interested, no problem."

She stared into my eyes for a second or two. "You want to chat with me?"

"I promise to be civilized. If you're nervous, you can bring an ashtray with you."

"All right," she said, having given it whatever thought she

felt it required. "I have a break in about fifteen minutes." She started to walk away, then added over her shoulder, "Try not to get drunk."

•

I went back to watching the customers, five distinct individuals homogenized by alcohol, then separated again by the same poison into a resigned solitude. They had the look of regulars, but ignored each other, content to mind their drinks. Anything they might have had to say to one another had long ago been drained of interest. Their lives now consisted of the paced administration of a general anesthetic.

Even without the booze in their blood, they were not an appetizing bunch. Not to my taste at all. There are vampires who will drink anyone's blood. Others who prefer the blood of one sex over the other. Some prefer children. Some fancy specific human types, like intellectuals or athletes. Others dine on specific ethnic groups, believing their blood to possess some desirable quality. For me, it was strictly a matter of practicality. All those subtle distinctions had a serious drawback. The pickier a vampire is, the harder it is to find a suitable meal. And in the final analysis, the connoisseur's subtleties are mostly pretense. It's just a way of trying to make something meaningful out of quenching a thirst. More to the point, it's just a way of trying to make their lives meaningful. As if the blood of a French female violinist or a teenaged Korean math prodigy might distinguish the belly that digested it.

Still, I had my own preferences, though they tended to be negative. I preferred to avoid the blood of the physically ill, including that of long-term drug users. A body ravaged by drug abuse is just as unpalatable as one ravaged by viral or bacterial infection. There wasn't any objective reason for my preference, since, as far as I knew, I was immune to human diseases. My reasons were purely psychological. I just liked to drink healthy blood.

I also tried to avoid feeding on kids under five or six years old, or on people over 60, or so. There was always an element of risk in killing humans. With few exceptions, people were always accounted for; if not by family and friends, then by the bureaucracies. When someone dies, someone else notices. If the death raises questions, someone always looks for answers. They may not look very hard or very long, but they still look. I avoided the young ones because there wasn't enough blood in their little bodies to justify the risk. It was more prudent to feed on larger bodies, getting a full nutritional return for the effort invested and the risk involved.

As for the old folks, I figured once a human reaches 60, they've earned the right to drag it out as long as they either choose to or can. They've fought a good fight against an unbeatable adversary in a battle that was lost from the beginning. As long as the old and gray weren't the only solution to my immediate dietary needs, I preferred to let them go their own distance.

Not feeding on small children was a matter of common sense, an attempt to minimize the chance of undesirable repercussions. My attitude toward the elderly was less obviously pragmatic. On the face of it, it was a curiously sentimental policy for a predator. But there was more to it than that. It grew out of a desire to invest the world with value. It was another of my many attempts to make the world meaningful by drawing lines around my own actions. I wanted to acknowledge that some things were better than others, and I wanted to respect the difference. At one level, I knew my distinctions were arbitrary. I really wasn't different in kind from a vampire who, for whatever idiosyncratic perversity, only drank the blood of twelve-year-old girls. We were both making arbitrary distinctions. And we were both trying to invest the world with value. We both needed to choose between the better and the worse, even if our choices were based on our own aberrations.

•

About fifteen minutes later, Karla came back to my booth and sat across from me.

"I guess you're not in the mood tonight?" she said, pointing to my untouched drink.

I responded by sliding the glass to the back edge of the table. We sat looking at each other. Beneath the pierced eyebrow, the multiple earrings, the tattoo of a goldfish on her neck, and the garish eye shadow, Karla was a classic Italian beauty: black hair, brown eyes, olive skin, with unusually symmetrical facial features. None of which had any real bearing on anything that concerned me.

"So, let's chat," she said.

I wanted to accomplish two things: to convince her to take

the job, and at the same time, I wanted her to understand that she would be making a serious decision, with serious repercussions if she broke the rules of her employment. Unfortunately, those two things worked against each other. If I gave her an accurate picture of the penalty for breaking the rules, I would eliminate any chance of her accepting the job. In the end, there was nothing to do but try.

"My name is Shake," I said, offering her my hand.

"Karla Lambretti," she responded, shaking my hand briefly and giving it a good squeeze. "That's an unusual name. Are you one of those oil sheiks?"

"It's Shake, as in, 'shake, rattle, and roll.'"

"Shake, rattle, and roll," she repeated. "Wow, I haven't heard that in a while."

"A little before your time, I guess. How about, 'shake your booty.'"

"I get the picture. So, what's this business matter you want to chat about?"

"Unfortunately," I began, "there isn't any way to make this sound entirely plausible, so I'll just explain the situation, and we'll see what you think."

"It sounds like I'm not going to believe you."

"You might not. But I'm not that concerned about whether you believe me. What I'm hoping is that you'll accept my offer, anyway."

"I've only got fifteen minutes," she said. "So whatever it is, you might want to get to the point."

"Let's start with the why. As luck would have it, I've been graced with a rather rare medical condition."

"Is it contagious?" she interrupted, leaning back.

"Not at all. It's genetic. It isn't especially debilitating, but it has one very inconvenient side effect: an extreme sensitivity to sunlight."

"You mean," she interrupted, "you're like a vampire, or something?"

"Nothing that fantastic. I'm more like a square peg."

"A square peg?" she asked.

I nodded. "You know, the square peg that won't fit into a round hole. In my case, the round hole is a normal life lived in the light of day. I have to stay indoors during the day and handle my affairs at night. For the most part, this isn't a problem. But occasionally things come up that have to be done during normal business hours. I'm looking for someone I can depend on to handle those for me."

"You want me to run errands for you?" she asked, her face clouding slightly.

"That would be part of the job, yes. I also need a chauffeur. I don't drive."

"Why not just take a cab? They work 24/7. Too expensive?"

"I'm not trying to cut expenses," I said, wishing to give her a better sense of my priorities. "I'm looking for someone I can depend on."

She sensed my change in tone and turned her attitude down a notch. "Why me?" she asked, soberly. "You don't even know me."

"It's true," I agreed, "I don't know you. But, to tell you the truth, I was impressed by the way you handled yourself the other night at the motel. Does that seem odd to you?"

"Well, since you ask, yeah, pretty fucking odd."

"It's not, if you think about it. I live an idiosyncratic life. When I need assistance, it makes sense to consider someone who also has a somewhat unorthodox life style. The person I'm looking for can't have a husband, two kids, and sell real estate on the side."

"So, what? Like, tending bar and turning tricks on the side are the qualifications you're looking for?"

"Not necessarily. It's more a matter of how you go about it. Let's just say I like your style."

She mulled this over for quite a while, staring at me the whole time, as if there was something in my face or expression that would help her decide what to do. This was enough for me to see she was interested and would soon get to the inevitable question. I gave her the time she needed, which wasn't much.

"What's the money like?" she asked.

Money wasn't a problem for me. I had a lot of it, and when I needed more, it was relatively easy to get. What wasn't so easy was finding someone who would do a good job for reasons other than money. Or, at any rate, not only for the money. It wasn't easy to find someone whose personal integrity, even their sense of well-being, didn't function like a puppet hanging from the strings of their greed.

"The money is good, and the job isn't complicated. You'd be my chauffeur, and run errands as needed. Beyond that, you're not to discuss me or anything you do for me with anyone else. And, as far as possible, you should try to refrain from asking too many unnecessary questions."

Karla thought for a moment, then nodded her head. "These errands I'll be running, are they legal?"

"Prostitution isn't legal."

"That's got nothing to do with it."

She was right, it didn't have anything to do with it. "I won't bullshit you, Karla. There may be an element of risk at times. But I won't involve you directly in anything illegal. And I'll look out for you. That may sound somewhat... how shall I put it? ...anemic, right now. But you'll see that it isn't. I'm not a bad guy to have on your side."

I didn't expect any of this to make a favorable impression on her. There wasn't any context for her to evaluate what the advantages or disadvantages might be. But she was used to taking risks.

"So what about the money?" she asked.

"I'll pay you a base salary of five thousand dollars a month, in cash. Always and only cash. In addition to the base salary, I'll pay a bonus for every occasion in which you chauffeur me, and a bonus for every errand you run. The amounts of the bonuses will be entirely at my discretion. They will not be negotiable." I paused to let her play with the numbers.

"Five thousand a month, plus bonuses?" she confirmed.

"Does that sound like something you'd consider?"

"I'll consider it," she said, trying not to smile. "How often will I be driving you and running errands?"

"That's unpredictable. There may be times when a month will pass without hearing from me. If that happens, you'll receive your base salary for that month. More likely, I'll need errands run two or three times a month, and I'll need you to drive me somewhere once a week, or so. That's a rough average. There may be periods when I need you more often, possibly even for several days running."

"Can you give me an idea of how much the bonuses would be?"

"I can, but I'd rather not. I'd rather you work for me for a month or two, and see how it goes. Are you willing to do that?"

She gave the appearance of considering it, but it was obvious her mind was already made up. "I guess so," she said. "How is all this going to work?"

"Does that mean you'll take the job?"

"Does that mean you're hiring me?"

"Yes, but you have to say to me, 'Shake, I'll take the job.'"

She gave me a quizzical look, then shrugged her shoulders. "Shake, I'll take the job."

"Good. Do you have a cell phone?"

"No. Do I need to get one?"

I took a cell phone, a set of car keys, and an envelope out of my coat pocket and placed them on the table. "The cell phone is for you. You don't need to worry about phone bills. They'll be paid for you. You do need to keep it charged and with you at all times, 24/7."

"Okay."

"Not some of the time, Karla. All the time."

"Okay, all the time."

"When I need you, I'll call you on that phone. If I need you for an errand, I'll give you instructions then. If I need you to drive me somewhere, I'll tell you when and where to meet me."

She picked up the phone, opened and closed it a couple of times, then set it back down. "Are those car keys?"

"They are. Do you know how to get to the corner of Fair Oaks and Manzanita?"

"Yes."

"There's a repair shop there called Tony's. Go there tomorrow morning and ask for Tony. Tell him you're there to pick up Shake's car. He'll probably look at you like you're nuts, or something. Tell him Shake asks how Linda is doing."

"Linda?"

"His daughter. He'll have the car brought out to you. It's registered to Tony, but it's yours to use as you please. Except, of course, when you're on duty."

"What kind of car is it?"

"A Dodge Magnum."

"Sounds macho."

"It may be, for a station wagon. It doesn't have many miles on it, so go easy for a while, until the engine's broken in. Have the oil changed regularly, and all that. By Tony. Likewise with any repairs. If you're not sure about something, just take it to Tony. Not to a different garage. Only to Tony."

"And I can drive it anytime I want?"

"As I said, it's yours to use as you please. But don't forget who you're working for and what takes precedence."

"Got it. You say jump, I jump."

She said this as a joke, but I wanted her to understand it wasn't a joking matter. "If you already resent the arrangement," I said, "we're not going to get along, Karla."

"Sorry," she said, sheepishly. "I'm not used to being at someone else's beck and call."

"Now is the time to say so if you can't do it."

She was staring at the car keys, holding them with both hands.

"Yes or no, Karla?"

She put the keys in her pocket. "Yes."

It was what I wanted to hear. "You're driving an old Honda, right?"

"It's not so old."

"If you want, you can sign the pink slip over to Tony when you pick up the new car. He'll sell it for you. He'll take a cut off the top for his trouble, but he's fair and he'll get a good price for it. Of course, that's up to you."

This seemed to satisfy the car question for her. "So what's in the envelope?" she asked.

"Our last order of business for tonight. Do you have a computer?"

"Yeah, more or less. It might be older than my car."

"What kind of computer is it?"

"An old desktop PC."

"Do you prefer a PC?"

"No, not really. I don't know very much about them. I got it cheap from a friend."

"There's five thousand dollars in the envelope. Tomorrow, after you pick up the car, go to the Apple Store at Arden Fair and buy a laptop. I recommend you go top-of-the-line, the seventeen inch MacBook Pro, but it's up to you. Have them fill it with RAM and buy the warranty. It'll run around four thousand. Use the remainder to buy a decent carry bag and anything you might want to add. Software, or whatever. What's left over you can keep."

She hadn't hesitated picking up the cell phone or the car keys, but she was looking at the envelope like it might bite.

"One thing you'll learn about me, Karla, I don't like to beat around the bush."

"Funny you should put it that way," she said. "I mean,

that's a lot of money, on top of the salary and the car. I guess I'm wondering how often you're going to be beating around my bush?"

I was glad she'd brought it up. "Your suspicions are understandable," I said. "So let's get it straight now, and we won't have to talk about it again. There won't be any fucking in this relationship. Neither literal nor metaphorical. I'm not going to fuck you, and as long as you're straight with me, and do your job, I won't fuck you over."

She was trying to be cool, but I could see the whole thing was a bit much for her.

"You know how weird this is, don't you?" she asked. "I mean, out of the blue, offering me this job, all this money?"

"What? Do you want to go home and fetch a copy of your resume? Do you want me to ask you a few standard job interview questions? How were your grades in school? Ever been arrested? Use drugs? Where do you see yourself in five years? Would that make you feel better?"

"You can say whatever you want. It's still weird."

"It is what it is, Karla. The job isn't difficult, but there isn't a lot of room for screw-ups. If you follow the rules, we'll get along peachy and I'll make it worth your while. If you don't, well, hopefully we won't ever have to go there."

She picked up the envelope. "I have to get back to work."

"I'll give you a call on Saturday," I said, and watched her walk away.

5

I knew there was a good chance that Francine Arnaud had merely imagined a connection between Ron Richardson and her husband's murder. Many of the events we perceive to be related are, in fact, not related at all. Their connections are completely imaginary. Like the man who thinks he's going to have a good day because he hits all green lights on his drive to work. At the same time, while our imaginations are misleading us, there is an inconspicuous web of subtle influences threading its way through the world, establishing a pervasive connectedness that passes largely unperceived. Between those two lies the world of practical affairs where a quarter buys you so many minutes in a parking meter, and you know that your computer is better protected by anti-virus software than by prayer. But there are times when the barriers—between the imaginary, the mundane, and the mysterious—give way and we can perceive things that would otherwise remain hidden. When that happens, the imagination, instead of leading us into fantasy, can function as a conduit into the world's mysteries. Or, at any rate, into something interesting.

That's what I was hoping for from the Arnaud business. Something interesting. And if that didn't happen, it was at least a chance to fatten my bank account. I didn't need Richardson's money, but I didn't like to pass up an opportunity for easy income. And the more I thought about it, the more Richardson looked ripe for the picking.

Either way, it really didn't matter if the

Richardson/Arnaud connection turned out to be a dead end. There wasn't anything riding on it. I was just curious. Of course, there were other considerations; some good reasons for keeping my nose out of the Arnaud mess. Involving myself in the private affairs of one of my meals just wasn't very smart. My rule of thumb was "Eat and run." Take what I was after and walk away. The best insulator between myself and my donors was distance. Whether or not to pursue the Arnaud matter came down to which was stronger: my curiosity over a chance convergence of events, or my reluctance to deviate from my normal policies for self-preservation.

Not surprisingly, my curiosity won out. I didn't really understand why, but over the years curiosity had become a kind of life raft for me. Vampires often perish from the inability to give their activities a guiding context. They lose the ability to make efficacious practical judgments. For me, a certain fascination for the complexities of chance, awe before the world's infinite contingency, was probably as close as I ever got to finding a guiding context for myself. Pleasure in my own curiosity was as close as I got to feeling at home in the world.

This may not have been any more than a story I told myself, but it was a useful story. If I were human, the world of social relations would provide a context to find meaning in my activities. But I was on my own. On the one hand, free to have my own reasons for doing what I chose to do. But at the same time, condemned to finding those reasons for myself.

When Saturday rolled around, I called Karla as I had said I would. She had picked up the car and bought the computer. She was as excited about the MacBook as she was about the car. We exchanged email addresses. I told her I wouldn't use email very often, and then only for general matters without urgency, but asked her to check her mail once a day, or so, just in case. I also gave her instructions to pick me up the following evening at 11:00 p.m. by the footbridge on University Avenue. I had decided to have a talk with Richardson on money matters, and I would play the Arnaud factor by ear.

The next evening, I arrived at the footbridge a few minutes early. The night was clear and cool, with a light breeze. The moon was just a sliver, low on the horizon. A beautiful dark night. Karla was already there, parked directly across the street from the bridge. I went around the car and got in on the passenger side. She was wearing a stocking cap pulled down tight on her skull and a black leather jacket. She looked like she was on her way to unload a truck.

"Nice hat," I said. "Been waiting long?"

She ignored the remark about the hat. "Not long. Five minutes, maybe. Where to?"

Richardson had a piece of prime riverfront property out on the Garden Highway, not far from San Juan Road. "Take Howe down to El Camino and turn left," I said. "Then go all the way to the end where El Camino hits El Centro Road."

She thought about it for few seconds. "It would be faster to take 50 to I-5."

"We're not in a hurry. Let's go the slow way. How do you like the car?"

"It's a nice car. What's with Tony the mechanic?"

"What do you mean?" I asked, anticipating what was to come.

"He's a little scary, don't you think? He's like, bigger than my refrigerator. He looks like he could throw a car at you if he got mad enough. I mean, big guys don't usually bother me. But he's freaky big. I don't mean he's like a freak, or anything. Actually, his body is kind of amazing. It's like, perfectly proportioned, but huge."

As humans go, Tony was a little scary. He was Navaho, and big even by their standards. Six foot five, with the barrel-chested, narrow-hipped build not uncommon among his people. Tony had a slight scowl that made strangers think he was angry, but he wasn't. His face was just put together that way. He was a very friendly, gentle man.

"Tony's all right. Did he give you a hard time about the car?"

"Not at all. He seemed kind of short tempered until I told him why I was there. Then he started falling all over himself, being like, super-polite."

"Did you ask him about Linda?"

"Yeah. He said she was doing fine and she got accepted at UC Davis."

"That's good."

"He also asked how Mio was. Is that your wife?"

Tony was one of the few people who had some kind of established relationship with both Mio and me. For me, he was a mechanic and he supplied a car. For Mio, Tony occasionally provided a different kind of service. But I wasn't ready to discuss any of this with Karla.

"I think it was Montaigne," I said, shifting the conversation away from Mio, "who said that curiosity was a scourge of the soul."

"I'm not sure what 'scourge' means," Karla said.

Most people will try to hide their ignorance, even when it

means preserving it. I was beginning to think Karla might be OK. "Originally," I explained, "a scourge was a whip used to dispense punishment."

"So does that mean if I ask too many questions you'll whip me?"

She seemed about half serious.

"Think of it as my taking an interest in your soul," I said.

She looked at me like I'd said something bordering on repulsive. "You're not going to start getting religious, are you?"

"Karla," I said, chuckling, "you can ask questions. Just don't get miffed if I choose not to answer."

Our eyes met briefly, then Karla returned to her driving. When we got to the end of El Camino, I had her turn right, then left on San Juan Road. San Juan terminated at the Garden Highway, a levee road running along the Sacramento River. Between the river and the levee there was a narrow strip of land decorated with the mansions of some of Sacramento's more moneyed residents.

I directed her to pull over just before the stop sign. Karla pulled the car onto the shoulder and stopped.

"I'll get out here," I said, opening the door.

"Am I supposed to wait for you?" she asked.

"I'm not sure how long I'll be. Maybe an hour. Maybe two or three. I'll call you on your cell when I'm ready to be picked up."

Karla glanced around at the dark, empty fields. "There's not much around here, you know, and it's kinda late."

"There's a restaurant on the corner of 28th and J that's open twenty-four hours. Or, if you want, you can go home and wait."

"It'll take me fifteen or twenty minutes to get back here. Is that okay?"

"That's fine," I said, and got out of the car. The air was full of river smells. Karla pulled away, turning left and heading toward downtown. Her receding taillights were the only visible traffic.

My destination was only a couple hundred yards from the intersection. Richardson's house was constructed of rectangular sections of steel, concrete, and glass. It followed the ground's gentle descent toward the river, like irregular steps forming the facets of giant crystals. I particularly liked the broad expanses of glass. They made the lit up interior look like a stage set. A riding lawn mower sat parked in the shadow of a shed about twenty yards from the house. The seat looked comfortable, so, like a vampire farmer who has driven his midget tractor to the drive-in movies, I climbed on and proceeded to watch the show.

Richardson and a woman who looked about half his age were in the living room, watching a very large wall-mounted wide-screen TV. The woman was wearing pajamas. She had recently showered and her hair was wrapped in a towel. Richardson was still dressed in jeans, cowboy boots, and a garish Hawaiian print shirt. He was slouched down on the sofa with his legs stretched out, his boots up on the coffee table. A dog, it looked like a Golden Retriever, was sleeping on the rug nearby.

At this point in the game, I preferred to leave the woman out of it, so I just watched, waiting to see how things would develop. I knew Richardson went through women at the rate of two or three a year. If this one had been with him for a while, I figured they would be past the honeymoon stage, and there was a good chance they wouldn't go to bed at the same time.

I figured right. It wasn't long before the woman sat up, said something to Richardson, kissed him on the cheek and left the room. Richardson didn't even look at her. A moment later a light came on in one of the bedrooms. I could hear a hair dryer run for a minute or two. Then the light went out.

Richardson continued to watch TV for another half hour or so before aiming the remote and turning it off. When the TV went black, the dog perked up and they both went out the back door. I climbed off the lawn mower and began to circle around the house. When I got to where I could see him, Richardson was standing at the far edge of the lawn, where the grass ended at a slope dropping down to the riverbank. The dog was meandering around with its nose to the ground, looking for the right place to pee.

Richardson had his back to me and I was downwind from the dog. I sprinted across the lawn, hooked my foot under the dog's rib cage, and gave him a little flip that sent him sailing out into the river. The splash brought Richardson out of his reverie. Confused, he stood staring, trying to figure out why his dog had jumped into the water. I stepped up behind him and gave him a shove that sent him tumbling down the slope.

Grunting and cursing, Richardson rolled to a stop just short of the water. I was already down the slope when he started to get up, and I slapped him hard across the cheek. My open-handed slap sounded like a small-caliber gunshot against Richardson's face. It knocked him down, spinning him halfway around so that he landed hard on his left shoulder. I grabbed both of his feet, yanked his cowboy boots off, and tossed them into the river.

They must have been his favorite boots. When he realized

what I had done, he flew into a rage, charging me with his head down, roaring like a bull. I stepped out of his path and slapped him again, hard on the back of the head. He went back down with a loud humph, his face and chest plowing into the dirt. Before he could try anything else, I put my foot on the back of his neck.

"Stay down," I commanded. "If you try to get up, I'll throw you in the river."

The fight went out of him as fast as it had flared up. "Please don't," he pleaded, "I can't swim."

I moved a couple of steps back and sat down on a rock. I could hear the dog breathing as it swam. The current had taken it a good way downstream before it found a spot to climb onto the bank. The tags on its collar jingled as it shook the water out of its coat, then the dog's padded steps headed back in our direction. A few seconds passed before its head appeared at the top of the slope. It made a little whining noise and retreated back to the house.

Disgusted by his dog's performance, Richardson apparently decided it was time to deal with the situation. "What the fuck do you want?" he asked, trying to make it sound like he was in control.

"I haven't even introduced myself," I said, "and you're already swearing at me, Ron."

Richardson rolled onto his side. "So who the fuck are you?"

"My name is Shake. And before you let your bad judgment get the better of you, if you try to attack me again, not only will I throw you in the river, I'll break both of your arms first. Are we clear on that?"

I could tell from the expression on his face he wasn't going to risk it.

"Those were five hundred dollar boots," he whined.

"Are we clear, Ron"?

"Yeah, we're fucking clear."

"Good. You can sit up now and we'll have a civilized conversation."

Richardson raised himself to a sitting position. "You mind if I use my handkerchief?"

I gestured for him to go ahead. He took it out of his back pocket and proceeded to wipe the dirt off his face.

"I'm going to say some names, Ron, and I want you to tell me what you know about them."

I recited the names of the three main distributors in his drug operation. When I said the first name, Richardson paused for a second, then continued wiping his face, as if it hadn't meant anything to him. On the second name, he stopped wiping his face. On the third, he looked like he'd swallowed the handkerchief. I waited while he decided what line of bullshit he was going use.

"Never heard of them," he said, as if that might settle the matter.

"The thing is, Ron, you can't actually play dumb if you really are dumb."

His anger flared again. He clearly wasn't used to this kind of exchange. "Do you have any idea who the fuck you're calling dumb?"

"A run-of-the-mill asshole who's been lucky, so far. I can change that if you insist."

"What do you want?" he asked, frustrated that his normal

blustering wasn't working for him.

"Don't you mean, what the fuck do I want?"

"OK, what the fuck do you want?" he corrected, putting on a show of accommodation.

"I want two things from you," I said, "neither of which is negotiable." I took a small slip of paper from my pocket and held it out close enough for Richardson to lean forward and take it without getting up. "That's a Cayman Islands phone number. Tonight, after we've finished our talk, I want you to call that number and ask for Mr. C. They'll ask who's calling. Tell them you're calling on behalf of Shake and you want to make a deposit. They'll give you instructions on how to continue."

"Make a deposit?" Richardson asked, curious about what that implied.

"Yes, Ron. From now on, on the last day of every month, you're going to deposit ten thousand dollars into my bank account."

Richardson scoffed. "You're out of your fucking mind!"

"The last day of the month, every month, before midnight, Pacific Standard Time. It's important that you not be late."

The idea of parting with that much money seemed to give Richardson a fresh shot of testosterone. "You listen to me," he yelled, starting to get up, "you insane little fuck! You don't..."

But I already had him by the throat. He started thrashing around, trying to free himself from my grip. I squeezed hard enough to really scare him. I thought his eyes might pop out of his face.

"I told you not to get up, Ron."

Richardson's eyes were jumping around in their sockets. He couldn't talk, but he made some sputtering noises. I let go of his throat and sat back down. "As I was saying, it's important that you not be late. Not even five minutes. If you're late, well, I'll have to do business with the asshole who takes your place."

"Business!" Richardson blurted. "This is what you call doing business?"

"A man who makes his living the way you do is in no position to put too fine a distinction on things."

"I can't..."

"Don't even start with that." I said, holding up my hand to stop his excuses. "I know how much money you make in a year. What you're going to pay me is little more than an inconvenience. A psychological inconvenience, at that. I know you hate giving anything to anyone if you can't take back twice as much. I know you're going to do everything you can to avoid paying."

"What the fuck do you expect?"

"I expect you to resist. And then I expect you to pay."

We looked at each other for a couple of minutes.

"You ever watch 'Star Trek'?" I asked.

"Jesus fucking Christ!"

"Answer the question, Ron. Were you a 'Star Trek' fan?"

"I wasn't a fucking Trekkie, if that's what you mean. But, yeah, I watched it."

"Do you recall what the Borg used to say to their victims?"

Richardson thought for a few seconds. "Resistance is futile."

"Very good. Resistance is futile. That's where you're at, Ron. Don't be stupid. You're not Captain Picard. Make your monthly deposits and learn to live with it."

"I can't fucking believe this. You expect me to give you a

hundred and twenty grand a year for nothing?"

"Ten thousand a month, by midnight, Pacific time, the last day of every month. Beginning this month, by the way. Since today is the twenty-ninth, your first deposit is due day after tomorrow."

Richardson wasn't used to being coerced by someone who wasn't backed by an organization more powerful than his own. And even when he didn't hold all the cards, he always occupied a bargaining position that would guarantee him a return on any compromises he might find it expedient to make. So I was fairly certain he wouldn't make the first payment. He'd want to test me, confident that he could counter any threat I was capable of presenting. That was fine. I could deal with that when the time came. For the moment, there was still the matter of Arnaud. I had told myself I was going to play it by ear, and apparently some part of me had come to a decision about what that meant.

"Now, the other little favor you're going to do for me."

"There's more?" Richardson asked calmly, as if I had already exceeded his ability to process audacity.

"About a year ago, a cop named Dean Arnaud was killed in a motel in Vacaville. Executed. Do you know anything about that?"

"I didn't have anything to do with that," he said, with enough conviction that I thought he might actually be telling the truth.

"Be that as it may, I want a name. If not the name of the guy who pulled the trigger, then someone involved."

"Jesus Christ, man! I don't know who the fuck killed him. I told you, I didn't have anything to do with it."

"You're a resourceful guy. Not all that smart, but you

know how to collect favors. Maybe you'll have to throw some money around. Whatever. I don't care how you do it, just get me a name by Friday."

"You can't be serious."

"Friday, Ron. There's a lot of cold, deep water out there."

I was done, for the time being. When Richardson turned to look at the river, I went up the bank and back into the night.

●

There were some riverfront condominiums a mile or so down the Garden Highway. About halfway there, I called Karla and told her to pick me up in front of the condos. She pulled into the parking lot a few minutes after I got there, coming to a stop with the passenger door at my fingertips.

"Everything go okay?" Karla asked.

"Well enough, I think."

"Where to?"

"Back to the university footbridge."

"Should I go back the way we came?"

"It's up to you."

Karla put the car in gear and exited the parking lot toward town.

"Did you find something to do while you were waiting?" I asked.

"I went to that restaurant you mentioned. Had a Denver omelette and read my book."

"Sounds yummy. What are you reading?"

She glanced briefly my way, as if questioning my motivation for asking.

"I'm just curious," I said.

"I thought curiosity was the scourge of the soul?"

"Only if you have one."

She laughed. "*A Frozen Woman*. It's a novel by Annie Ernaux."

"You like it?"

"Yeah. I like the way she writes. Very sparse. No gushing emotions, no irony. She just tells you what it was like. Her life. Growing up in a small town in France. How it was both beautiful and stifling. How she loved and hated it. She makes you understand what she had to go through."

"Sounds interesting."

"Also, I guess I kind of fell in love with her photo on the back."

I wasn't sure how to respond to that.

Karla slapped the steering wheel with the palm of her hand. "Fuck! I can't believe I said that!"

"Don't sweat it," I said. "I did the same thing once, became interested in an author after seeing his photo on the back of one of his books. I ended up reading everything he wrote. Walter Abish. He wears an eye patch."

When we were nearing the footbridge, I told Karla to pull over and park for a minute. When she stopped and turned off the engine, I unzipped my fanny pack and removed an envelope.

"What's this?" she asked, when I handed it to her.

"Sixteen thousand dollars. Normally, I'd pay you on the last day of the month. But it's the twenty-ninth, and I won't be needing you again this month, so I'm paying you tonight, for the full month. Five thousand base salary, five hundred as a bonus for picking up the car from Tony's, and another five hundred for tonight. That's six thousand. Is that agreeable?"

Karla looked incredulous. "You're not shitting me, are you?"

"The other ten thousand," I said, "is for future expenses. Don't waste it, but don't hesitate to use it if the need arises. Carry some with you. A thousand or two. That's important. Don't come to work with empty pockets. When that runs down, let me know so I can give you some more. Also, if I were you, I wouldn't put it in the bank. At least not in one lump sum. The banks are required to report deposits over ten thousand dollars."

"Right," she said, thumbing through the bills, "taxes."

"I'm not positive yet, but I'll probably need you to drive me somewhere Wednesday evening. I'll call you on Wednesday and let you know, one way or the other."

I opened the door and started to get out, pausing when Karla said my name.

"Yes?" I asked, leaning down and looking in the door.

"You don't live under the footbridge, do you?"

"I'll talk to you on Wednesday. Good night, Karla."

"Good night, Shake," she said, after I had closed the door.

6

My tolerance for human company diminished over the decades as I gradually adjusted to a life of solitude. This was partly out of necessity and partly because I simply lost interest in people. There were exceptions, of course, but they were few and far between. Even when I did cross paths with someone who sparked my interest, interaction with humans always required a level of detachment that tended to preclude all but the most superficial relations. For one thing, I knew for certain that whatever novelty or enrichment a human might offer, it would soon fade. People quickly betray their limitations. And when you add to that the difference in human and vampire life spans, people came to seem like fleeting diversions. Like pet goldfish, they were colorful, but it was never very long before they went belly up.

I suppose my attitude was a little cold-blooded, but a certain amount of misanthropy went with the territory. It was impractical to be too sensitive about one's food. The relationship of eater and eaten imposed the need to maintain a clear, categorical distance. Paradoxically, the need to function in human society required the opposite; the cultivation of pragmatic social skills. These two conditions worked against each other, with a vengeance. My century-long path to a workable solution had been thorny, unpredictable, and not without moments of comedy.

After Calvin and I climbed out of the rubble in 1908, there was a decade or so during which the novelty and the inherent excitement of my new life served as a counterweight to a host of less appealing conditions, including my newly acquired and growing aversion for human company. It was a time of exhilarating exploration of my vampire powers. I reveled nightly in my senses, time and again astonished at what I was capable of. By moonlight, I could read the dial of a watch on the wrist of a man standing thirty paces away. I could hear the heartbeats of every man, woman and child in a crowded room. And if I chose to, I could isolate a given rhythm and identify the heart's owner. I had the nose of a bloodhound, and could track like one. The world of scent became a redolent olfactory kaleidoscope.

Initially, I might add, this kaleidoscope was not all roses. Wild animals are not offended by "bad" odors, because they haven't been socialized to distinguish good odors from bad. Odors are just odors. If a dog sniffs something caustic or acidic, it will reflexively pull away, but not because of any idea associated with the smell. A dog has no problem with bad breath, stinking feet, farts, or any other special effects of the human body. A vampire's reactions, on the other hand, are vestigially human, at least until he has had time to unlearn them. Before that happens, crowds of humans can leave a newly turned vampire gasping with incredulity.

But as impressive as my vampire powers were, they were not really supernatural. I could not, for instance, outrun a bullet. A vampire is subject to physical laws—inertia, gravity, and so on—just like other creatures. I could run about forty-five miles per hour, tops. Which is to say I could, if the need arose, chase down an ostrich. This is considerably faster than the fastest human, but it is still the running speed of a two-legged animal. As for stamina, if I had to, I could maintain thirty miles per hour for a couple of hours. And I could jog along at twenty all day. Or rather, all night.

Naturally enough, adjusting to my heightened powers brought its little problems. It took me quite a while, for instance, to get used to my own strength. For a long time, I inadvertently broke things. I had to relearn how much effort to invest in common tasks, like lifting objects that were no longer heavy. I would open a door and find the knob snapped off in my hand. I broke so many shoelaces I stopped untying my shoes when I took them off.

I also had to make some radical adjustments in how I dealt with people. Even the most formidable were no longer threatening. The difference in strength made it ludicrous for a human to offer physical resistance. Nor was it just a matter of strength. My reflexes were unmatched by any animal I'd ever encountered. But again, this didn't mean I could dodge bullets. I may have been able to anticipate a bullet's trajectory. I could see that someone was pulling the trigger of a gun pointed in my direction, and in the time it took the finger to squeeze, I could probably move out of the way. But this ability was dependent on my seeing the gun being fired. A bullet in the back, though it wasn't likely to kill me, would definitely spoil my mood.

Even after a hundred years, I'm still occasionally surprised to discover some previously unsuspected talent. But these tend to be small surprises. For the most part, I know what I can and can't do. What I can't do is tolerate sunlight. It is genuinely unpleasant. I can survive maybe twenty seconds of direct exposure. Maybe. I have never been inclined to test that particular limitation. Discovering my strengths was usually more entertaining that bumping up against my weaknesses. And often enough, discovering what I could do forced me to deal with the consequences when my curiosity, my enthusiasm, or my boredom got the better of my judgment. These failures of judgment often began as small things, seemingly trivial when first committed. Then the consequences would start to snowball and it would soon be obvious that I had once again gone too far.

A good example comes to mind. I was in a small town near Atlanta, Georgia. It was in 1919, I think. I was strolling one evening among the crowd at a county fair. In one of the booths, a "strongman" was challenging all comers to arm wrestling matches for twenty-five cents, and doing pretty well for himself. He was a big guy, rather obese, but with a lot of muscle under the fat. I watched him easily defeat a well built young man, taking a lot of pleasure in laughing at him afterwards and taunting the other male bystanders to show their wives and girlfriends what they were made of. It was just part of his act. He would ridicule his audience, trying to shame them into paying a quarter to prove themselves.

It was stupid and pointless of me to make a spectacle of myself in front of all those witnesses. It would have been okay if I'd lost the match. People would have understood that I'd just wanted to try. But they could not understand my winning. I'm five feet ten inches tall and weigh about one hundred fifty pounds. I was several inches shorter than my opponent and about half his weight. His upper arms were thicker than my thighs. Of course, the size difference was irrelevant. No matter how strong the guy was, he had the strength of a human. The match was legitimate only as a contest between two men. With my vampire strength there was no contest.

Looking back, I can only assume I was bored out of my

mind. I stepped forward and slapped a quarter onto the tabletop. The strongman got a good laugh when he saw me, and of course the crowd was equally amused. Rather than side with an obvious loser, most of bystanders immediately switched allegiance, calling out for the strongman to break me like a twig, and other charming encouragements.

We squared off across the table. At the signal to begin, we both held our arms in place without applying any pressure. He looked at me, smiling, waiting for me to press. I looked at him, not smiling, waiting for him to do the same. We stayed that way for maybe thirty seconds before he began to slowly add pressure, as if he were conducting an experiment to determine exactly how much I could resist. I matched the gradual increase, just enough to keep my arm vertical. At a certain point, when it became clear to him that what was happening wasn't possible, he gave it everything he had, straining until his lips began to quiver and the veins bulged out of his neck and face.

The crowd had gone dead silent. Not betraying the least effort, I winked at the strongman, then perfunctorily forced his arm down and pinned the back of his hand firmly against the table, then stood up and walked away from the murmuring crowd. I continued to stroll aimlessly through the fairgrounds until my mistake became undeniable. Once again, I had drawn too much attention to myself. People were watching me, pointing me out to others. It was only to be expected. They were there for entertainment, novelty, a temporary respite from the monotony of their lives. By failing to keep my distance, by failing to remain detached from human affairs, I had played right into something potentially dangerous. I left the fair, and the next night I left Atlanta.

At that time, my dilemma was still working its way forward in my mind. My relationship to humans was neither simple nor natural. People may have been my primary source of nourishment, but they were not toys. They were neither passive nor harmless. In fact, they could be pretty nasty. All my new vampire powers were exhilarating, but they could also get me into trouble if I didn't learn to control them.

7

A large sum of cash has its own gravitational field. It pulls violence into its orbit. Violence itself didn't bother me. But the more volatile a situation is, the more unpredictable it becomes. I was never injured during one of my little drug-money heists, but the possibility of gunplay was always present and luck could have worked against me.

That was all back in the days when I needed money. I often put a lot of work into the process of acquiring it, something that I needed as much as I needed the cash. Planning my thefts gave me something to do, a way to occupy my time. But over the years, having appropriated and invested several million dollars, I found myself less and less entertained by the whole process.

That's where people like Richardson came in. The more I lost interest in the process of acquiring wealth, the more I liked the idea of someone just giving it to me and saving me the trouble. Or most of the trouble, anyway. The thing about people with money, the more they have, the more they invest in keeping it, and the easier it is to shield themselves against those who would like to take it away from them. The rules attached to wealth are a kind of game, and one of the rules is that the richer you are, the more immunity you enjoy when you break the rules. Which is to say, the more freedom you have to make up the rules as you go along.

In Richardson's case, I was fairly certain he wouldn't willingly play by my rules. He'd do what came naturally to him. He'd beef up his personal security and the next time I showed up, he would try to take me out of the game. People like him, accustomed to the prerogatives of wealth and power, always have to have their little fists pried open. But that was all right. I was good at applying leverage.

I checked my Cayman Islands account early Wednesday morning. As expected, no deposit had been made. That evening, I gave Karla a call and told her to pick me up at the footbridge at 1:00 a.m. I didn't want anyone near Richardson's place to see me, so I had Karla drop me off in the condominium parking lot where she'd picked me up the previous Sunday. From there, I made my way to Richardson's on foot.

I approached the house through a wooded area that separated Richardson's property from his up-river neighbor. The garage door was open and a car—probably his girlfriend's—was parked inside. Richardson's Jaguar was parked out in front of the garage, and there was a Hummer parked next to the Jag. Most likely, the Hummer came with bodyguards, and the choice of vehicle suggested a concern with image that may have taken precedence over professional competence. Or maybe not.

The first thing I needed to do was find out how many there were. I worked my way around to the front of the house. The living room was unlit, but the kitchen light was on, illuminating the large living-dining-kitchen area. A long, high counter separated the kitchen from the larger part of the room. There was a guy sitting on a stool at the counter, reading a paperback. He was big, probably six two or three, a little overweight, but he looked like he spent a lot of time at the gym pumping iron. He was also wearing a shoulder holster.

I made a complete circuit of the house. There was one other hired hand sitting in a deck chair on the unlit back porch.

This guy was smaller, slender, and alert. His head leaned back against the chair cushion, so his face was tilted slightly upward, but his eyes were open. His hands were clasped loosely in his lap and his feet were planted flat on the deck. He looked like he took his job seriously, and I suspected he might be the more capable of the two.

I moved further back into the surrounding woods. The small fanny pack I was wearing held an extra long-sleeved, black t-shirt like the one I had on, some heavy-duty plastic cable ties, and a woven-leather blackjack. I took out the blackjack and looped my left hand through the strap, then moved a little closer to the house, but still well back in the shadows. I wanted to take both guards out of the picture at the same time, so I had to wait for them to get closer together.

I watched the guy in the deck chair for about forty-five minutes. He only moved once, when a large rat came up from the river, crossed the yard and disappeared under the house. The guy's eyes followed the rat's progress, his head turning slowly as the animal meandered across the yard. Humans aren't usually very good at waiting. If they have to do it quietly, especially if it's dark, they'll usually fall asleep within a few minutes. This guy was still alert.

A little over an hour had passed when the big guy stepped out to the porch. There was an unlit cigarette in his mouth, which he lit after sitting in one of the deck chairs. The smaller guy had his back at a forty-five degree angle to the wall of the house. The big guy sat to his right with his back facing west toward the river. I wanted to approach from behind the smaller guy, so I moved around to that side of the yard.

As a general rule, I didn't kill except for food. That's why

I'd brought the blackjack. I was waiting for the big guy to turn his head to the east, so he wouldn't see me approach. When he finally turned, I came out of the woods along the back wall of the house, up onto the deck, and gave the smaller guy a tap with the blackjack. He went limp in his chair. I stepped behind the big guy and paused, a little surprised he hadn't heard anything. When he turned back and saw his partner slumped in his chair, he chuckled. It was probably the first time he'd ever caught him sleeping on the job. The big guy took a slow, meditative drag on his cigarette, as if enjoying his partner's lapse of professionalism.

"Frank," the big guy said, conversationally. Then again, "Frank," a little louder. He leaned forward, reaching out to shake his partner's knee. I could have watched more, but I was there for other reasons, so I clocked him on the back of the head and he rolled forward onto the deck. I took out two of the cable ties and bound their feet, then dragged them both off the porch and into the woods, out of view from the house. I tossed their guns and searched them. The big guy didn't have any other weapons, but Frank had a small tactical knife sheathed on his belt. I put it in my fanny pack, then turned them onto their stomachs and bound their hands behind their backs. As a final precaution, I positioned them back to back and looped another cable tie through the two already on their wrists. If they woke up before I was finished inside the house, this would make it harder for them to move around.

Once inside the house, I made my way to the open door of the master bedroom. From the doorway, the bed was on the left, centered against the wall, with nightstands on both sides. The room must have been about four hundred square feet. It made the over-sized bed look smaller than it really was. Richardson was asleep on the near side of the bed, his girlfriend on the far side, with about three feet of empty space between them. Ron's dog was sleeping at the foot of the bed. I stepped into the room, moving to the left of the doorway, and made a little clicking noise with my tongue. The dog raised its head, looked at me for a second or two, then very slowly got up and walked the perimeter of the room, keeping the maximum possible distance between itself and me, until it came to the doorway. I could hear it picking up speed as it ran down the hall.

Richardson had failed to make his first monthly deposit, and now there was a penalty to be paid. It wasn't fair to make the woman pay for Richardson's bad judgment, but, as so often happens, expediency ruled the day. Or in this case, the night.

I went around to the woman's side of the bed. The room was warm. The blankets were pushed down to her waist. She was laying on her right side, her back to me, the left side of her bare neck offering itself. She groaned quietly when I bit into her, tensing for just a second before her body relaxed again. When she was dead, I wiped my face with the sheet and went around to Richardson's side of the bed. Richardson was lying on his back with his mouth open, snoring like an asthmatic. There was a large crystal bowl full of m&m's on the nightstand. I scooped up a few, then sat in an armchair against the adjacent wall. I tossed one of the m&m's in a gentle arc. It landed with a faint tap on Richardson's forehead. He twitched, but didn't wake up. The next one landed in his open mouth. It must have gone deep into his throat because he choked and bolted up to a sitting position, hacking. The m&m shot out of his mouth onto the bed.

"Fuck god!" Richardson half whispered, feeling around on the sheets for whatever had been in his mouth. Then abruptly giving up the search, he flopped back down on his back.

The next one hit Richardson on the cheek. This time he was awake. He flipped onto his right side, brushing the pillow frantically, as if something alive and unwelcome and been on his face. When he saw me sitting in the chair, an explosive hiss came out of his mouth as he pushed himself backward and up onto his right elbow. He must have backed into his girlfriend's body, because he glanced quickly behind him.

"Don't worry," I said. "You aren't disturbing her."

"You!"

I smiled, got up and switched on the lamp on the nightstand, then sat back down.

"How the fuck did you get in here?" Richardson hissed.

"Your guards left the back door open."

That got Richardson thinking. His eyes darted over to the nightstand, then back to me.

"What's in the drawer?" I asked, glancing toward the nightstand.

Richardson was trying to add it up. How fast could he open the drawer and get the gun? Would I be fast enough to stop him?

"Don't be an idiot, Ron." I got up casually and opened the nightstand drawer. There was a chrome-plated .357 Magnum in a leather holster next to a box of condoms. I didn't generally get any pleasure out of being callous, but my intention was to create a certain impression on Richardson. That is, I wanted to scare the shit out of him. I sat the condoms on top of the nightstand. "You can fuck her now without these, Ron."

Richardson rolled over and looked at his girlfriend. He must have stared at her body for a full minute before looking back at me. I had sat down again, the .357 resting on my knee.

"You killed her, you motherfucker!"

"The way I see it, you killed her, Ron. When you failed to make the bank deposit."

"I'm not giving you all that money."

"If you're serious about that, if you really aren't going to pay me, then you should repeat what you just said, and I'll kill you now and spare us both any additional inconvenience."

I waited for him to think it over. I noticed his eyes moving now and then to the door.

"Your boys are taking a little nap in the woods," I said. "If you're still alive when I leave, you'll probably want to go out and cut them loose. They can help you get rid of her body."

"I loved her, you fucking asshole!"

"She was trophy snatch, Ron, like all the others, and you know it. You'll replace her in a week."

"Goddamnit! You can't do this to me! You just killed a woman. I'll make sure you burn for it."

"Don't get sidetracked. What about the bank deposit?"

"You're really going to kill me if I don't give you the money?"

"I am. I already told you that. This is your last chance. You didn't take me seriously the first time, and it cost your girlfriend her life."

Richardson turned his head and looked at her body lying inert beside him. He moved several inches away from her, as if her death had immediately reduced her to something distasteful, something he did not want to touch.

"Are you getting the message, Ron?"

Richardson was like a little kid who'd spent a long time

convincing himself he could fly. Then someone came along and pushed him out of his tree, and of course he hit the ground like the sack of shit he really was.

"I'll pay you, goddamnit!"

"It's Wednesday. Well, Thursday morning, to be precise. I'll give you until midnight tonight to make the deposit. Are we agreed on that?"

Richardson nodded his head in the affirmative.

"Now then," I said, satisfied that the money issue was settled, "what about Dean Arnaud?"

The expression on Richardson's face told me everything I needed to know. "You didn't do your homework, did you, Ron?"

"What the hell, man! I told you I didn't have anything to do with that."

"I have reason to think you know something about it."

"Yeah?" he said, forcing disdain into his voice, like a man unsure of how convincing his lies are. "What reason would that be?"

Finding Richardson's photo in Francine's closet didn't necessarily mean he had anything to do with the murder, but I wasn't going to give him the benefit of the doubt. One way or another, everything a man like Richardson said was a lie. "We've come a long way tonight, Ron. I think we've really started to understand each other."

"Jesus Christ! I'm telling you the truth. I didn't have anything to do with killing that cop."

I picked up the .357 and opened the cylinder. It was fully loaded. I removed one round and examined it, as if evaluating its suitability to the task at hand, then replaced it and closed the cylinder. I raised the gun and pointed it at Richardson's head. He winced.

"But you know something about it, don't you?"

"Look, I admit I'm in the drug business. So what? So are the fucking pharmaceutical companies. Anyway, the asshole wasn't killed over dope. Not as far as I know, anyway. He was snooping around, asking questions about some missing girl. Somebody didn't like it, so they got rid of him."

"What's the connection to you?"

"There isn't any fucking connection. Arnaud bought dope sometimes from one of my people. That's all."

"Arnaud was dirty?"

"It wasn't a fucking secret. You want my guess, that's why his murder was never solved. The guy was an embarrassment. The cops didn't want the bad press."

"Did he buy the dope for himself?" I asked.

"Some, maybe. But I think he sold most of it. Small time shit. Convention goers, people like that, out-of-towners."

"So what makes you think he wasn't killed over dope?"

"I don't know, it's possible, I guess. But it doesn't make sense. He was too small-time."

Richardson was the one not making sense. People were killed every day for a lot less than Dean Arnaud was carrying. "There's more you're not telling me, Ron."

Richardson tried to look offended.

"What I'm curious about is why you seem to know quite a bit about Arnaud, but you say didn't have anything to do with his murder."

"Arnaud bought some coke from my guy, a couple grand worth, the same day he got popped."

"And you know this because?"

"My guy got nervous when he heard about Arnaud trading the dope for a bullet in the head."

"So what did you do?"

"I didn't do anything. I told my guy to shut the fuck up and forget about it. As long as the police didn't know who killed Arnaud, there wasn't any problem."

I smiled at Richardson. He didn't smile back. He seemed to be waiting for the obvious.

"What's your guy's name?" I asked.

"Goddamnit, I don't need this shit stirred up."

I didn't say anything, just waited, tapping my index finger lightly on the barrel of the 357.

"Danny Weiss," Richardson said, after about half a minute. "He lives over in West Sac. His address is in the fucking phone book."

I knew there was more Richardson wasn't telling me, but it was time to go.

"About your girlfriend," I said, aiming the gun at her corpse. "You'll want to dispose of the body so it won't be found."

"Maybe I should just call the police when you go."

"Believe me, Ron, you don't want the coroner to do an autopsy. If they determine the cause of death, they'll crucify you."

Richardson looked again at his girlfriend's body, as if he were trying to calculate just how much trouble she could cause him.

I took the bullets out of the gun and tossed them across the room, then dropped the gun on the floor and kicked it under the bed. I got up and walked to the door, pausing before going out. "You should go check on your bodyguards."

"Fuck them! They deserve to spend the night out there."

"I'm not sure what the big guy is worth, aside from the fact that he's big and mean-looking. Frank is probably worth whatever you're paying him."

"Yeah? Why'd he let you in here, then?"

The question didn't even merit a response.

●

I called Karla and instructed her to pick me up in the parking lot where she'd dropped me off. Something was nagging at me on the walk back; a feeling that had become all too familiar in recent years. A sense that my actions were somehow out of balance. I didn't quite understand the feeling, but, as usual, I knew what caused it. I had used his girlfriend as a convenient tool for coercing money out of Richardson. This bothered me in a way that was very difficult to understand. It was not a matter of immorality or injustice. I was a vampire, a predator that required human blood to survive. I was not at odds with that. Nonetheless, I couldn't help feeling that I had somehow failed to properly discriminate. I had made a decision in a situation that offered the possibility of greater balance, and I had not made the right choice. I had exploited an opportunity for blood without weighing the options. I had taken something for granted that I shouldn't have. I just wasn't sure what it was.

I could hear something Euro-synthish on the car stereo

when Karla pulled into the parking lot. She turned it down as I got in.

"How'd it go?" she asked.

"Could you turn that down a little more?"

"Don't like Miss Kitten?" Karla asked.

"Miss Kitten?" I repeated, enjoying the name. "I have to confess, I haven't been following her work."

"She really tickles me. I think she used to be a stripper before she broke into the music scene."

"I see," I said, having no reason to think the move from strip club to recording studio wasn't a natural one. "The lyrics are amusing."

"So, how'd it go?"

"It went all right, I think."

"I guess you wanted to surprise him? Or her?" she asked, tentatively.

"Him," I said, and waited, not expecting that to satisfy her curiosity.

"That's why you had me drop you off on in the parking lot, right? You wanted to surprise him?"

"If one of us was going to be surprised, I preferred it to be him."

"Was he?" she asked, after a short pause.

"I believe so, yes. How was your evening?

"Not too exciting. I went home after I dropped you off."

"You sounded like you were asleep when I called."

"You could tell?" she asked, sounding slightly disappointed.

"Your voice was a little lower than normal."

The streets were empty. Downtown Sacramento had an air

of bleak desolation at night. City planners, people whose greed was only matched by their lack of vision, had tried various schemes over the years to "revitalize" the core. They generally got a lot richer in the process, while everything else got poorer. They had added a performing arts center and a convention center, but after about eight p.m., the surrounding streets remained distinctly uninviting.

"Is this city creepy at night, or what?" Karla said, having similar thoughts.

"I may have some errands for you in the next few days," I said, "I'll either call or email."

She dropped me off at the footbridge. It was still early, time for a leisurely stroll home. I wondered if Richardson was right about Arnaud not being killed over drugs. But why would he be killed over the missing girl? I decided that was a question I would ask Danny Weiss.

8

My current residence was a gift from Mio: a two-story house on American River Drive, about a mile from the university. I occupied the four upstairs rooms: study, kitchen, bedroom, and bathroom, with a private entrance at the back of the house. The ground floor was occupied by Keiichi Sato, a Japanese gentleman employed by Mio to live in the house, take care of the grounds, and maintain a discreet indifference to me. Sato performed his duties impeccably. He and I rarely saw one another, and when we did, we just as rarely spoke. On those occasions when our paths crossed, more often than not we would acknowledge one another's presence with nothing more than a slight nod of the head.

Mio's relations with humans were not usually based on affection, but in Sato's case, I think she was genuinely fond of him. She once told me how they had met. It was back in the 1980's, during Japan's economic bubble. Mio was walking very late one evening through Tokyo's Ueno Park. Her path took her towards a solitary man sitting on a bench, staring lifelessly into the darkness. At first, she thought he was one of Japan's countless salarymen for whom alcohol was the only refuge from the subservient monotony of their lives. But as she passed in front of him, he came out of his reverie and asked her very politely why she was walking alone so late at night. His speech was very precise, not at all slurred by drink. She replied that she was on her way home. He stood up and offered to escort her through the park.

Mio thought it was considerate of him, but wondered if he had ulterior motives. When they exited the park, rather than pursuing some tedious male perversity, he politely enquired if she would be able to continue safely without his assistance. She assured him she would be fine. He thanked her for the conversation during their walk, and did so with such charm that she asked him for one of his meishi, his business cards. Later, she had one of her associates look into Sato's situation. As it turned out, Sato's wife had recently been killed in an automobile accident. He was very attached to her and the shock of her sudden death had been too much for him. He suffered a breakdown, stopped going to work and was eventually given an early retirement. As far as anyone knew, he spent most of his time wandering aimlessly around Tokyo, often sitting all night in parks.

With her typical perspicacity, Mio saw in Sato someone perfectly suited to her needs. She approached him with an offer to spend his retirement in California, as the caretaker of her house in Sacramento. He accepted the offer with obvious gratitude, and has lived here ever since.

Mio had lived in the house for a couple of years before deciding that Sacramento was not to her liking. When she had first bought the house, she brought a crew of craftsmen from Japan to make modifications to the interior. There were, in fact, five upstairs rooms. The fifth room was a narrow area between the bedroom and study, about six feet wide, running the full length of the two adjoining rooms. This hidden space was where I routinely spent my daylight hours. If you didn't know it existed, you would never suspect that the study and bedroom were separated by more than an intervening wall. Access was via a fiendishly clever hidden door in the study.

Mio referred to it as the shoebox, and for lack of a better name, so did I. It was furnished with a narrow but quite comfortable bed, a small freezer in which I kept an emergency supply of blood, a comfortable lounge chair, a bookcase with a few dozen of my favorite books, and a desk with a computer. There was another computer in the study, equipped with a broadband Internet connection. The two computers were connected via a router, and there was a surveillance camera that allowed me to view the study from inside the shoebox.

In addition to the hidden entrance, an emergency exit was concealed beneath a throw rug. Lifting the hatch gave access to a ladder leading down a narrow shaft that descended, hidden on the ground floor behind cabinets, to a tunnel under the house. The tunnel led underground about fifty yards to another concealed hatch in the floor of a shed in the back yard.

When Mio first showed me the house, she explained that the emergency exit had been built mainly in case of fire. I learned later that fire was a particularly sensitive issue for her. Mio was born in 1765, in Edo, now Tokyo, the daughter of a minor government official who had distinguished himself by drinking and gambling away the family's modest fortune and, along with it, their respectability. When she was fifteen, her father, in financial distress, indentured her to a successful Edo doll merchant. As it turned out, the merchant himself had no personal interest in Mio. He had been acting as a proxy for someone else. That someone else was a rich and eccentric doll maker named Midori.

Hinamatsuri, the doll festival, dates back to Japan's Heian period, sometime before the twelfth century. Dolls created by the more celebrated craftsmen were, and still are, prized as works of art and often fetched large sums from collectors. Midori's dolls were generally regarded as among the very finest. In addition to being a respected artist, she also happened to be a vampire; a lonely vampire in search of someone to relieve her solitude. Mio proved to be the perfect companion. Once turned, Mio understood immediately that Midori had rescued her from the humiliation and drudgery that awaited her as the daughter of a disgraced petty bureaucrat, and she was deeply grateful.

The psychological life of vampires can be complicated. On the one hand, they are separated from humans by inescapable disparities. Most of what distinguishes a vampire from a human being makes an equitable relationship close to impossible. A vampire has to conceal too much, and the need for secrecy makes the relationship one-sided, emotionally constrained, and unsatisfying. On the other hand, although it is possible for two vampires to form deep and enduring bonds, it rarely happens. We always seem to be too volatile to mix. But there are exceptions. Mio and Midori lived together for seventy years and, to hear Mio tell it, they were absolutely dedicated to one another. When their time together ended, it was not the result of incompatibility.

In the early 1850s, they were living in a country house on the island of Kyushu. More than anything else, Midori's untimely end was due to her own carelessness in arousing the superstitious fears of the peasants living in the surrounding villages. For reasons Mio was never clear about, rumors began to circulate through the villages that Midori was some kind of demon, responsible for a variety of local misfortunes. As happens with rumors, they were progressively magnified in the retelling, eventually becoming so outlandish that they either had to be dismissed outright, or taken as true. Dismissal was by far the less interesting option, so it wasn't long before community consensus took its natural course in the form of a mob.

Luckily for Mio, the prevailing opinion was that she was an innocent victim ensnared in Midori's evil web. The village where they lived was about a half day's journey from the city of Fukuoka. Mio and/or Midori made periodic trips to the city to deliver dolls to the merchant who handled their sales. The trip, of necessity taken at night, required a one day layover. Whoever made the journey would spend the intervening day at a house owned by Midori on the outskirts of Fukuoka.

Wishing to spare Mio, the vigilantes waited for her to make one of those periodic trips. On a sunny August afternoon, about two hundred villagers surrounded and set fire to their house. Midori was sleeping in a specially darkened upstairs room. The house, old and made entirely of wood, was quickly engulfed in flames. According to what Mio was later told by witnesses, Midori had thrown a blanket over herself and run out of the house into the sunlight. Once outside, she found herself surrounded by angry villagers armed with long spikes and other weapons. Having escaped the fire, she was now exposed to the even more deadly sun. She tried to get through the mob and make a break for the surrounding woods, but in the confusion she couldn't find a way through. Desperate to get out of the sun, she retreated back into the burning house.

Vampires don't die easily. Her screams could be heard for so long that many of the villagers fell into a kind of mass hysteria, screaming and wailing, terrified that Midori might emerge from the flames and take vengeance on them.

Midori's fate exemplified an ever-present danger. Over time, there is a tendency to become complacent, a natural tendency to tempt fate by pushing your luck. The more you get away with, the more you feel you can get away with. But sooner or later, your carelessness catches up with you. When it does, you pay the price in one lump sum, at the point where you've gone too far. You get away with it until you don't, and then it's too late. Vampires are not, in fact, immortal. Caught in the wrong circumstances, we are much weaker and more vulnerable than humans. Which was a large part of why I cultivated a life of quiet anonymity, why I was so cautious about moderating and disguising my culinary activities. My vampire blood may not have pulsed in rhythm with my domesticity—prudence, discretion, patience, and the like, may be rather tepid virtues, more appropriate for a work-a-day family man than for a vampire—but the routines gave my life a certain stability that was preferable to the alternatives.

9

As Richardson had said, Danny Weiss was in the phone book. He lived on Cummins Drive, near the Lighthouse Golf Course. There were a lot of new homes being built in the general area, but most of the older houses were small and rather run down.

I wasn't comfortable yet involving Karla in anything too potentially compromising, and since I had no idea what might transpire during my visit with Danny, I decided to ride my bike. I liked riding a bicycle. I could make good time without drawing attention to myself. A cyclist doing twenty-five miles per hour is well within the realm of human expectation. Also, a bike was fairly easy to hide if I needed to leave it somewhere.

A little after midnight, I rode through town, crossed the river at the old I Street Bridge, and made my way to Cummins Drive. There were two cars in Danny's driveway: a late model BMW and a classic Ford Mustang. A faint glow from inside suggested lights further back in the house. The street was quiet, so I leaned my bike against the side of his house, behind some shrubs.

The backyard was fenced with the ubiquitous six-foot redwood. Twin gates shared the space between Danny's and his neighbor's house. I put my hands on top of Danny's gate, jumped, swung my feet over the top and landed quietly on the other side. Of course, there was a dog—drug dealer standard issue—a big male Doberman. It came around the corner of the house, alert and pointy-eared, snorting with fearless disdain. It paused for about half a second and then charged. Two strides and it was airborne with unquestionably carnivorous intent. I let its head get a couple of feet from my face before I snapped my right hand up and grabbed it by the throat. The dog's forward movement stopped like it had hit a wall, but the momentum carried its tail end forward. I side-stepped and let the momentum flip the dog belly up, then slammed the back of its head down hard onto the concrete walkway. So much for fearless disdain.

I walked around to the back of the house. A roofed patio with a sliding glass door gave entry to a dimly lit family room. The right side of the room was occupied by a makeshift entertainment center: a wide-screen TV and stereo components flanked by two massive speakers. Danny's neighbors must have loved him. On the left side of the family room, instead of a family, a young girl slouched unconscious on the sofa. A guy, Danny no doubt, was kneeling in front of her knees, in the process of removing her panties.

The door wasn't locked. I slid it open quietly and stepped inside. "Are you familiar with the term, 'consenting adult'?"

The guy spun around so fast he lost his balance and ended up on his butt between the girl's knees.

"Because I don't think she qualifies as either," I added.

The coffee table, pushed aside, was littered with drug paraphernalia. The guy's eyes flicked over the tabletop, reflexively evaluating the extent of incrimination, then moved to the open back door.

"Your puppy is napping," I said.

Danny stared at me, but with unfocused eyes, like he was trying to remember something useful from all those hours he'd spent imagining how he would handle an intruder.

"Take a breath, Danny, before you pass out."

Saying his name brought him back into focus. "Do I know you?" he asked.

"I don't think so."

An ottoman sat against the wall, next to a bookcase. I walked over and casually examined some of the titles before sitting down. I had my back to Danny while I was looking at the books, curious to see if he would try something heroic. He didn't budge.

"You going to college?" I asked.

Danny puffed disdainfully through his nose. I wondered if that was something he'd learned from his dog.

"Man, what do you want from me? Why are you in my house?"

Danny was a fashionable little rodent. It looked like he spent most of his spare time shining his very expensive Italian shoes, and the rest of his time experimenting with his hair and glasses, trying to look less like a hamster.

"Don't be so touchy," I said, pointing to the girl. "I see you're a connoisseur of the arts of seduction. I was just wondering if you're a scholar, as well."

Danny remembered the girl's knees flanking his shoulders. "Shit!" he said, as if he thought I had been paying him a compliment, "This bitch is too stupid to seduce."

I couldn't deny the possibility that Danny was right. "She's what, about sixteen, seventeen?" I asked.

"I don't know," he said, dismissing the question. "She's old enough."

"Old enough to be drugged and raped?"

"Hey! I didn't drug her. She did that herself."

"You just sold her the drugs and then decided to take advantage of the situation?"

"What are you, like, her dad, or something?"

Danny didn't appear to be suffering from any moral dilemmas. If I wanted to do a service to humanity, drinking this little prick's blood would probably qualify.

"Nothing like that. I'm just trying to get a sense of who I'm dealing with."

"Anyway, who says I sold her anything?"

"I know who you work for, Danny." I said, casually examining the paraphernalia on the coffee table.

"You here to score?" he asked.

"Just information, Danny. Tonight I want to get high on information."

I heard the faint hiss and smelled it before Danny realized what was happening. Finally, with a funny, inquisitive expression on his face, he cranked his head around, staring between the girl's legs. "You little bitch!" he screeched, then jumped up, grabbed her by the wrist and yanked her off the sofa. She hit the carpet with a thud but didn't wake up. "The cunt pissed on my new sofa!"

Gawking at the wet stain, Danny started to shift his weight like he was going to kick the girl.

"Don't," I said, with enough force to stop him.

He looked at me, trying to decide if he had to obey. "Whatever, man!" he said, stepping back. "This little bitch just ruined my new sofa."

"Danny!" I said, "Forget the sofa."

His eyes jumped back and forth several times between me

and the girl before it sank in that maybe his sofa cushion wasn't his most pressing concern.

"Here's what I want you to do," I said, pausing for a little dramatic effect. "I want you to sit in her pee."

"What?"

"You heard me. Sit down in her pee."

"No fucking way, man. What the fuck?"

"I'm not asking, Danny. And I'm not going to say it again."

We looked at each other while the seconds ticked by. In the end, Danny shrugged his shoulders as if to imply that there was nothing he'd enjoy more than to relax in her urine. He tried to be sneaky at first and sit on the edge of the wet spot. I motioned him over with a wag of my finger, and Danny scooted obediently into the dark stain. A sick expression clouded his face as the dampness soaked through his pants.

"Now that we're comfortable," I said, "about a year ago you sold some cocaine to a cop named Dean Arnaud, who subsequently got himself killed. Do you remember that?"

"How do you know about that?" Danny asked, genuinely surprised.

"Let's not get sidetracked. Who was Arnaud going to sell the dope to?"

Forgetting about the pee, Danny put his hand on the cushion, then jerked it off again like he'd been burned. "Fuck!" he said, wiping his hand on his pants. "I don't know shit like that. He pays for the product, it's his. I don't give a shit what he does with it."

"How long were you dealing to Arnaud, before he was killed?"

"I don't know. A couple years."

"So you knew each other pretty well?"

"No, we didn't fucking know each other. He was a customer. That's all."

"He never talked to you about what he was doing? Who he sold to? Nothing like that?"

"Hey! The guy was a cop. Dirty or not, I didn't trust him and I didn't like him. I wouldn't have gotten near him if Richardson hadn't sent him to me in the first place."

"Richardson sent him to you?"

"The first time, yeah."

"And the last time?"

"Yeah, maybe. Now that I think about it, I guess he did say Richardson had set him up with a buyer. But he didn't say who exactly. Just some Russian guys in town for a Kings game, or some shit like that. Fuck, man! I can't remember all the shit I hear."

Richardson had lied about how much he knew, and Danny may have been making a lot of it up as he went along.

"Let me see if I'm following you, Danny. At first you didn't know anything, and now that you think about it, you just happen to remember that Arnaud mentioned some Russians?"

Danny performed a brief routine of innocent exasperation, as if to show me how little it all had to do with him. "Man, you know I can't just throw names around, even if I knew who they were. And I don't. Arnaud was always running his mouth about some shit or other. I got the impression he was selling the powder to these two Russian guys that used to come to town once in a while, that's all."

"How do you know them?"

95

"They used to by from me sometimes, back before Arnaud started playing middleman."

"What did they look like?"

"Like Russians, I guess. Big Russian dudes. One of them had a number tattooed on the back of his hand." Danny held up his right hand as he said this. "404. Except the second four was backwards, like a mirror image."

It was possible Danny was following orders from Richardson about what to tell me, and Richardson wanted to steer me toward these Russians. He probably thought they could get me off his back.

The girl was still breathing, but she hadn't moved from where Danny had thrown her off the sofa. "Who's the girl?" I asked.

Danny looked at her like she was as irritating as the pee he was sitting in. "A customer. Nobody, really. Just some fucked up rich chick."

"You use this shit?" I asked him, pointing to the drug paraphernalia on the coffee table.

"Fuck no, man. That's for stupid people. It's strictly business."

"And young girls."

"Whatever, man."

Danny just wasn't a very likable guy. That, in itself, was not a reason for me to kill him, but the circumstances were offering me a convenient meal, and that was a reason.

"So, you hungry?" I asked, as if we were old buddies who might step out for pizza.

Danny looked confused.

"Hungry?" I repeated. "You want to get a bite to eat?"

Danny started to laugh, but tried to hold it back, making a choking sound that escaped through his nose. "No I don't want anything to eat. Jesus!"

"You don't mind if I grab a bite, do you?"

"Whatever, man."

So I did. I drank about a quart, then held Danny down on the sofa and let rest of his blood mix with the girl's pee. When he was almost dead, I went through the kitchen drawers and found a small screwdriver and used it to stab Danny a couple of times in the neck to disguise the teeth marks, then cleaned my prints off the screwdriver.

The young girl had beautiful hands. Slender and very soft. The nails looked like they'd been done professionally. The cops were going to have fun figuring this one out. I pressed the handle of the screwdriver into her palm. She surprised me by gripping it, like an infant grasping its mother's finger. She was a minor. She'd get off easy. Maybe the ordeal would help her clean up her act. Or not.

I went into the bathroom and washed my face and hands. There was some blood on my shirt, so I took it off and buried it on the bottom of Danny's overflowing laundry basket. I put on the spare I carried in my fanny pack, then left the house, sliding the back door closed on my way out.

The connection, whatever it was, between Arnaud and Richardson was puzzling. It may have been limited to whatever drug-related business transpired between them, but I had a hunch there was more to it. Richardson would need a good reason to put a cop, no matter how dirty, between Danny and his customers. I had no idea what that reason might be, but it could have had something to do with the missing girl. Maybe.

Or maybe not. Maybe the Russians killed Arnaud for reasons that had nothing to do with Richardson. Maybe Arnaud had been killed over something related to the missing girl and Richardson's role was just to set up the drug buy. It was possible Richardson didn't even know in advance that Arnaud was going to be killed.

I was going to have to dig a little deeper.

10

____

Karla had only been working for me for a few days, and I wanted to give her time to get settled into the job. I thought I'd have her drive me a few more times, run some errands, and so on, before I started expanding her duties. As it turned out, our next evening drive wasn't as routine as I'd intended.

I gave her a call and asked her to pick me up at 11:00 p.m. at the footbridge. The night was breezy and overcast, but it didn't feel like rain. Karla was right on time. Her outfit wasn't as blue-collar this time. She was wearing her leather jacket over a light sweater, but no hat. She was also wearing makeup: lipstick and eye shadow, and what she probably thought was a subtle touch of perfume. To my vampire nose, the touch wasn't so subtle. Fortunately, it wasn't one of those modern androgynous scents that suggest an attempt to market youthful innocence in the guise of debauchery. Or was it debauchery in the guise of innocence? Either way, this particular fragrance was something from the chypre family, with a hint of patchouli, which I rather liked.

The evening's destination was a rural area northeast of town, around Sloughhouse. It was far enough away from the city that there was still pastureland with small herds of horses and cattle. A mammal as large as a horse or cow has enough blood in its body that a few pints can be drained off without causing the animal any harm. The careful incision of a leg artery produces an abundant flow of blood, and coagulates soon enough not to endanger the animal's life. Not that I was concerned about the animal's life. It's just that a dead horse attracts the owner's attention and scrutiny, whereas a small cut will most likely go completely unnoticed. Which means I can go back to the same herds again and again without arousing suspicion.

My intention was to have Karla park somewhere convenient and wait in the car while I slipped into a nearby field to practice my bloodletting arts. We took Watt Avenue south, turned east on Jackson Road, then south again on Sloughhouse Road. A mile or so further, there was a stand of eucalyptus trees where a creek crossed under the road. The shoulder there was wide enough to park the car and the fields on both sides of the road were used to graze a few horses and cattle.

"I won't be long," I said, opening the door. "Maybe fifteen minutes. You should keep the doors locked while I'm gone."

She looked around, trying to imagine what we were doing parked in the middle of nowhere, but she didn't ask. I heard the locks click after I'd shut the door. When I was far enough away from the car to be sure Karla couldn't see me, I hopped the fence and moved quietly toward a group of six cows, four of which were lying down near a feeding trough. These were dairy cows, which tended to be fairly placid and would usually allow me to approach without losing their wits, if they happened to have any. I chose one of the two standing cows, approached it slowly, then rubbed its flank to calm it. With a small ceramic knife I'd brought along for the purpose, I made an incision on the inside of the left front leg. I had taken a couple of pints of blood when I saw the lights of a car coming from the north down Sloughhouse Road. The car slowed as it passed Karla, but continued on south.

If I would have been paying more attention, I would have

seen the lights abruptly go out further down the road. I did hear a car door open and close, but the sound came from well south of where Karla was parked. I should have been more cautious, but I went back to my dinner. A couple of minutes later, I heard voices, one male and one female, talking quietly, then the sound of Karla's car door opening. I stood up and sniffed the air, catching the scent of Karla's perfume, and then a different scent. A male scent.

I jogged back to the road, then walked quietly toward our car. The driver's door was open and a man was standing against it, preventing it from being closed. I could see Karla's profile through the rear window. She was leaning away from the open door, as far as she could without climbing over the center console. As I began to catch the guy's words, "...matter, baby? You can't spare a little?" I picked up my pace.

He was reaching in with his right hand, trying to take hold of Karla. I could hear the fear in her voice, hissing "No!" as she tried to brush his hand away.

"You want me to hurt you, I guess," he said, reasonably, as if it were her intention rather then his.

He let go of the door and started to go after her with both hands. As he bent down to extend his reach, I tapped the rear fender with my knuckles. He turned his head, froze momentarily when he saw me, then slowly stood up, turning to face me. He was apparently sure enough of himself to smile. The degree of miscalculation behind that smile almost made me laugh. I thought of a story by Chuang-tzu, one of the two Taoist sages, about a praying mantis in the road. As it is about to be crushed by the wheel of a carriage, it raises its arms in a posture of threat. The little critter just didn't get it.

When the guy stood up, Karla scrambled over the console and out the passenger door. She stumbled a few steps away from the car before spinning around. I glanced at her calmly, which seemed to confuse her. Her eyes darted back and forth between me and the guy, but she didn't say anything, just stood there breathing hard.

"This your daddy?" the guy asked Karla, but without taking his eyes off me.

"Shake," she whispered.

The guy took a large folding knife out of his pocket, opened the blade, and held it out in front of him to give me a good look. He had definitely watched too many movies. "We can do this the easy way," he said, "or the hard way."

I wondered how many times he'd fantasized about using that line on someone. Who knows, maybe it was his favorite line and he used it a lot. He was quite a bit bigger than me, broad and muscular and no doubt mean as hell.

"Since you're offering us a choice," I said, "what's the easy way?"

"The easy way," he said, "is you get in your car and drive away and forget any of this happened."

"And the hard way?"

The pleasure he took in describing the hard way suggested his preference. "The hard way, fuck head, is I gut you and then me and the girl take up where we left off."

I looked at Karla. She was wide-eyed. The guy had given her a bad scare. If I let him walk, the whole experience would be so negative for her, she might decide to quit. I thought I'd better give her a clearer idea of who was on her side.

"Let's do it the hard way." I said.

There was a moment of surprised confusion before he smiled even wider. He stepped away from the door and circled out into the street so that, facing him, I had my back to the car. He was waving the knife back and forth in some way he must have thought was threatening. I was pretty sure we'd both seen a lot of the same movies, so I raised my hands a few inches, palms up, and gestured with my fingers for him to come forward. The smile disappeared, his eyes narrowed and he came at me, swiping the knife at my face.

I caught his knife hand by the wrist, forcing it out away from our bodies. With my other hand, I grabbed a handful of his jacket and pulled him in close, holding him immobile against his effort to pull away. Our faces were only a few inches apart. I held him there, watching the bravado draining out of his eyes, replaced first by confusion, then by fear. I was squeezing his wrist, slowly increasing the pressure, giving him time to let the disbelief sink in. He dropped the knife and screamed with pain as the bones in his wrist snapped.

"Down," I said, lowering him, "on your knees."

When the knife hit the pavement, I heard Karla exhale, then her footsteps coming around the front of the car. She stopped a few feet away, her fists pressed to her chest, as if she were shielding herself from something. She was hyperventilating and I was afraid she might pass out.

"Karla, why don't you sit in the car."

She looked at me, at the car, at the guy on his knees, then lunged forward and spat at him. I'm not sure any of her spit hit him, but she sprayed me pretty well. This seemed to satisfy a need that allowed her to relax some, and she sat down behind the wheel, leaving the door open so she could watch.

The guy was cradling his right arm against his stomach. I rapped him on top of the head with my knuckles to get his attention. "What's your name?"

He looked up at me. He was crying. "Bill."

"How's your wrist, Bill?"

"You broke it!"

"Life can be so unpredictable, can't it? I mean, one minute, you're just minding your own business, living your life as best you can. The next minute, something horrible comes along: a disease, a freak accident, it could be anything. Maybe you're sitting in your car, waiting for a friend, and some evil, predatory freak decides to terrorize you."

The strain of trying to figure out what was happening had stopped his crying. "I'm sorry. I wasn't going to hurt her."

"Shit like that, Bill, is only going to make it worse for you."

I turned and looked at Karla. She was still shaking, but her breathing had settled down. "He says he's sorry. Should we forgive and forget?"

"Break his other arm!" she said, with enough venom that it seemed to surprise even her.

"You hear that, Bill. She doesn't think your apology comes from the heart. Would you like to try again?"

I'm always amused by how quickly the typical bully can shift into groveling and ass licking.

"I'm really sorry," he whined. "Really, really sorry. I don't know why... what I was doing. I'm such an asshole, sometimes. I can't help it. My life is complete shit. I don't know what's wrong. I just can't get..."

I rapped him again on the top of his head. "That's enough, Bill. You're supposed to be feeling remorse, not self-pity."

It just wasn't smart to let him walk away, but I didn't want Karla to witness the alternative. There was a telephone pole about twenty yards south of the car, close enough to be visible in the darkness. "You see that telephone pole, Bill?" I said, pointing.

He glanced in the general direction.

"I'll make a deal with you. I'll give you a head start to the pole. That's pole number one. The next one down the road is two, the one after that, three. If you can run to pole number three before I catch you, I'll let you walk away."

He was young and fit. He measured the head start in his mind and I could see his confidence rise. "If I don't make it, then what?"

"Then you don't make it." I said.

He looked at me like there was something more to say.

"That's the deal, Bill. I suggest you start running before I change my mind."

He scrambled up and took off, holding his damaged arm against his chest. Under different circumstances, his confidence would have been justified. For a human, he could really run. I glanced at Karla. She looked positively mystified. Then I took off after Bill. I wanted to time it so that I caught him a few strides before the third pole. When he passed the second pole, he looked back over his shoulder. The expression on his face was priceless. I was a lot closer than he'd expected, and he really turned on the steam.

I closed the gap. When he was just a stride or two from the pole, I nudged him on his right shoulder. Running flat out as he was, he had no control over the change in direction. The telephone pole was about six feet from the road edge and he hit it at full speed. The impact knocked the air out of his lungs and he bounced back several feet, landing flat on his back. I walked over and checked him. He was unconscious, but still breathing. I grabbed a handful of his jacket and shirt with one hand, and his belt with the other, picked him up, spun him around and slung him against the telephone pole. When I checked him the second time, he wasn't breathing.

When I got to the car, Karla was leaning her forehead against her two fists gripping the steering wheel. She had been badly shaken. She spoke without raising her head. "Is he gone?"

There wasn't any point in my trying to make light of the situation. She could either cope with it, or not. "He's about as gone as he can be."

She raised her head then, turning to face me. "Did you kill him?"

I was a little surprised at how cold the question was. She may have been afraid of the man, but she was not afraid of the answer to her question.

"Let's just say he came to a crossroads, and, as so often happens, he made the wrong turn."

"He was going to hurt me, Shake."

For a second I thought she was going to cry, but she didn't.

"I don't know if he was going to rape me, but I know he was going to hurt me."

"All things considered, you handled yourself pretty well tonight," I said. "I'm proud of you."

There was a faraway look in her eyes, as if she were struggling to square what I'd just said with the preceding events. "I don't think so, Shake," she whispered.

"I told you when we first met that I wasn't a bad guy to have on your side. I'll look after you, Karla. But you have to help. It wasn't smart to open your door to that guy."

"I know I fucked up, Shake. I'm sorry."

"I'm curious about something. This was the second time I've seen you spit on some guy. What's that about?"

She thought for a second, then laughed nervously. "A few years ago, I had this real shit for a boyfriend. We used to fight all the time. So one time, he said something that really pissed me off, and I punched him in the face. It was the first time in my life I'd ever really slugged someone. It wasn't like in the movies. I hit him as hard as I could and I broke my hand. It really hurt! And of course, the asshole got a good laugh out of it. So now I spit. That way I don't break any bones."

"You know, Karla, I like that about you."

She looked at me questioningly.

"Even when you're furious, you're never completely out of control."

She smiled, seemingly a little embarrassed, as if she wasn't quite sure to what extent it was meant as a compliment.

"Can you drive?" I asked.

She started the car, put it in gear, but gave it too much gas, spinning the tires in the dirt. She backed off immediately and started again, more slowly.

"You know," I said, "he might have had a gun. You had no way of knowing. In the future, if you should ever feel the need to drive away, if you feel it's your only alternative, then drive away."

"I thought I could handle it. You know, take care of myself, be the tough girl."

I thought again of Chuang-tzu's praying mantis. "You're tough enough, Karla. But strength is always relative to the context. He was a lot bigger than you. In situations like that, you have to be smart, too."

She was quiet for a minute. "He was bigger than you, too, Shake, but you..."

"You made a mistake with him. He made a similar mistake with me. Who knows? One day I might make the same mistake with someone else. We all tend to take too much for granted."

Karla drove in silence for a few minutes. "What you did to him... he didn't have a chance against you. Is this one of the things I'm not supposed to ask questions about?"

"Why don't you turn right on Jackson and just drive for a while. We'll take the long way home tonight."

———

11

I wanted to give Karla some time to think about what had happened. If she decided to quit, it was better that she do it now. I could cut her loose with a relatively easy mind. I decided not to call her for a week, or so. In the meantime, I could pay a visit to Hamilton Investigations, LLC.

With Richardson, I had been dealing with a man who had embraced corruption as a way of life, an all-around scum bag, someone practiced at intimidation, using it whenever it served his purposes. Violence, or its threat, was an integral part of his normal business strategy, maybe even a source of amusement. But intimidation isn't always the shortest path between two points. Hamilton Investigations called for a more discreet approach.

A few minutes on the Internet followed by a few nights of observation told me that Hamilton Investigations was a one-man operation, run out of the owner's home. David Hamilton, divorced, lived by himself in a modest house in a nondescript residential neighborhood just off Marconi Avenue. He seemed to spend most of his free time at a local watering hole, a bar called The Intermission.

It was time to take a closer look. I rode my bike to Hamilton's house, passing by The Intermission on the way to make sure his car was in the bar's parking lot. There wasn't any activity on the street around his house, so I coasted up the driveway, opened the gate to the backyard and rolled my bike inside. The door on the side of the garage was locked, but the handle was old and wobbly. I turned it until it stopped against the lock mechanism, then continued to turn slowly. The lock gave a little as it bent, then snapped. The latch bolt was still in the lock plate, so I got out my knife, slid the tip into the space between the door and frame, and worked the latch bolt free.

The garage was a mess. I looked around briefly, satisfied that the accumulated junk wasn't work-related, then tried the door to the house. It wasn't locked. Unlike the garage, the kitchen was tidy. A few recently washed dishes were stacked in a drainer next to the sink. Across the living room, a hall led to three bedrooms. The front bedroom was Hamilton's office. An old, beat up seven-drawer desk sat in front of the window. On the right side of the desk, two armchairs took up the remainder of the space along the front wall. On the adjacent wall, a movie poster hung over a coffee table: *After the Thin Man*, with William Powell and Myrna Loy. Two filing cabinets stood in the corner opposite the armchairs. I opened the top drawer of one of the cabinets and found a lifetime supply of paper clips, ballpoint pens, custom printed stickies, and other office essentials. The paper clips were particularly well stocked; enough to last a vampire's lifetime.

I closed the drawer and tried the other filing cabinet. This one held hanging folders labeled with clients' names. I found the one labeled "Arnaud," pulled it out and sat down at the desk. There wasn't much in the file: copies of a few receipts, the invoices Francine had paid, and two pages of yellow binder paper with hand-written notes like: 1st meet: 3/11. Husband killed. Dean Arnaud, cop. Drugs? Innocent? And so on. From what I could glean, it looked like Francine had wanted Hamilton to look into her husband's death for the purpose clearing him of any drug-related wrongdoing.

According to Francine, the reason her husband had been in Vacaville had nothing to do with drugs. He was there looking for their missing niece, her older sister's kid, who had disappeared several months earlier. A photo of the niece—it looked like a high school yearbook portrait—was clipped to the folder, "Miriam Moore" printed on the back. That much of what Richardson had told me was apparently true. From Hamilton's notes, it looked like Francine didn't know why her husband's search had taken him to Vacaville on the day of his murder.

Nothing in the file suggested any progress toward explaining Arnaud's death. There were a few other entries consisting of sentence fragments ending in one or more question marks. At the bottom of the second page, Hamilton had printed "Ron Richardson?" followed by "North CA drugs. Major Player?" Then some time later, with a different pen, he'd added the word "Bloodsucker," the same thing Francine had written on the photo I'd found in her closet. I wondered which of the two, Hamilton or Francine, had first used the word to refer to Richardson.

Coincidences have a way of proliferating themselves, compounding themselves, attracting more coincidence, like a spider building a web, until an interrelatedness becomes visible and tangible. This is really just a convenient way to think about it. The webs of interrelatedness are there all the time. We don't notice them because connections are mostly hidden in an overabundance of details, like the fibers hidden inside a rope. The only way to see the individual threads is to unravel the rope. Humans are generally too busy with the rope to be bothered with the threads. People have things to do, lives to live, responsibilities to attend to. Their very survival depends on their ability to filter out most of the inconsequential details and focus on their priorities. Life is short, so people attend to what they can. The rest becomes background noise.

Hamilton's priorities required him to do the opposite: unravel the rope to see where the threads went. But apparently he hadn't gotten very far. Conspicuously absent from his case notes was any mention of Danny Weiss. Which meant, I suppose, either Hamilton hadn't made the connection to Weiss, or that Hamilton didn't keep good notes.

I put everything back in the folder and returned it to the file cabinet. I went through the other drawers, but didn't find anything of interest. It looked like most of Hamilton's work was marital related surveillance. On my way out, I peeked through the living room curtains. The street looked quiet, so instead of leaving the way I'd come in, I walked casually out the front door, retrieved my bike and rode away.

12

Karla sent me an email the next evening.

Shake,
Ever use iChat?
KL

I was pleased to see that whatever conflicts may have arisen over the events in Sloughhouse, she was apparently able to resolve them in favor of keeping her job.

I wrote back:

Karla

Occasionally. My screen name is 'darkMatter.' Since I'm writing, I'd like you to pick me up at the footbridge on Thursday evening at 9:00 p.m. There's a movie playing at the Tower Theater I'd like to see. If you're not interested in watching the film, you can drop me off at the theater and pick me up when it's over. If you'd like to see it, you're welcome to accompany me. It's a Jarmusch film, *Broken Flowers*.

Shake

Thursday night was cold, with a light, steady drizzle. Karla was waiting when I got to the footbridge. I shook the water off my umbrella, closed it and placed it on the floor in front of the seat before getting in. I could feel her watching me.

When I looked, she was smiling.

"Hello, Karla."

"Hello, Shake."

"Is something amusing?" I asked.

She put the car in gear and pulled away. "I was just noticing how tidy you are."

"Tidy? Is that a euphemism for something?"

My question seemed to fluster her. "No, I didn't mean anything by it. I guess I'm just trying to figure you out."

"Making any headway?" I asked.

The expression on her face suggested she'd given it some serious thought. "None at all."

"Aitken Roshi says the point isn't to clear up the mystery, but to make the mystery clear."

"What's an aching roshi?" she asked.

"Roshi means old teacher. It's a term of respect used in certain Zen sects. Aitken is the man's name. Robert Aitken."

Her attention was taken up with driving as she accelerated onto the freeway heading downtown. After we'd merged into the flow of traffic, she returned to the conversation. "Are you a Zen Buddhist?"

"I'm more interested in the art than the religion."

"You could be, though. A Zen person, I mean. However you say that. I think that's kind of what I meant by tidy. Zen tidy, not like, I don't know... not anal-retentive tidy."

"Not to change the subject, but are you going to drop me off or come in and watch the film?"

"Come in, if that's all right."

"Good choice," I said. "Have you seen any of Jarmusch's films?"

"No, but after I got your email, I went online and read a review of *Broken Flowers*. And a little about Jim Jarmusch, too."

"I've been a fan of his since *Stranger Than Paradise*, one of his early movies, back in '84, I think. A bit before your time."

The Tower Theater and the Crest Theater on J Street were the only two remaining pre-mall-era theaters in Sacramento. They were the only two theaters that screened independent alternatives to the big studio productions. Developers had been scheming for years to tear the Tower down. But so far, community resistance had held off the wrecking ball. I didn't particularly like the theater itself. It was old and musty, though not entirely without charm. The staff, to their credit, hadn't been completely homogenized by a corporate image. They looked a bit fringe, leaning toward the gothic or grunge or something along those lines, which meant my own somewhat funereal pallor didn't raise eyebrows at the ticket counter.

It was the last show on a Thursday night, so there wasn't much of a crowd. I didn't mind crowds so much, but people sometimes unconsciously sensed danger in my proximity. It was probably something coded in their genes. Most of the time, they didn't even know it was happening, but their reactions were always tangible to me, like a very mild electric current in the air. I liked it, but it made me hungry, so it wasn't always expedient.

"Do you have expense money with you?" I asked Karla.

She was dressed in black, including black leather boots with heels that made her taller than me, and she'd done something spiky with her hair, which made her look taller, still. "Two thousand," she said, giving me a look intended to make it clear how unnecessary the question was.

"Would you mind paying for my ticket?" I asked.

115

"Okay, but if you want popcorn, you're on your own."

•

Afterwards, I suggested we go to a 24-hour restaurant. On the way, we talked a little about the film.

"I really enjoyed it," Karla said.

"I like Jarmusch's sense of humor."

"Yeah," she agreed. "Like the next door neighbor, Winston. What a crackup."

"The way he handled the letter mystery was very amusing."

"Yeah, the Bill Murray character, Johnston, acted like he couldn't be bothered, like he wasn't interested. But he really wanted to know who wrote the letter."

"The more I think about Johnston, the more complex he seems to me."

A slight smile pulled at the corner of Karla's mouth. "I know she only had a few seconds of screen time, but I thought Tilda Swinton was incredible. She's such an amazing actress. At first, I didn't even recognize her."

"Do you think she was the one who wrote the letter?" I asked.

"I don't know. I've been thinking about that. Probably, she did. But we don't really know, for sure. I like that, too. Not knowing for sure. The movie's better that way, I think."

"I agree. Penny, the Swinton character, seems like a good candidate for the letter writer. But there are little details here and there to raise your doubts."

Karla was quiet for a minute. "You know, I was a little nervous about going to a movie with you."

"Oh? Why is that?"

"I was afraid you were going to be one of those intellectual types who wants to, what do they call it, deconstruct it afterward."

I wasn't surprised to hear that she'd been nervous, but I was amused to hear the reason why. "I've watched a lot of movies," I said. "I don't expect to learn much from them, beyond perhaps something about the art of film making, which I'm not especially interested in. I go to the movies for the pleasure of the story, of watching it unfold. There are a few actors and directors I like, because I can usually depend on them to provide that pleasure. Beyond that, I leave the criticism to the people who get paid for their opinions."

"In that case," she said, after giving it some thought, "you can ask me to take you to the movies any time you want."

•

At the restaurant, we sat in a booth by the window facing J Street. I encouraged Karla to eat if she was hungry. She ordered a salad and I ordered a bottle of Perrier.

"Is that all you're having?" she asked.

"I have to be careful about eating in restaurants," I explained. "I have some bad allergies. Even in good restaurants the cook may not know what's in the food. In places like this, they don't even want to know."

"Is that why I've never seen you eat?"

"Partly. Why?"

"Nothing, really," she said, shrugging. "It's just, you know, nice to see people enjoy themselves."

"By watching them eat?"

"That's one way."

I was pretty sure Karla would not find watching me eat an endearing activity.

"You should be a politician," she said.

I waited for her to elaborate.

"You're good at sidestepping topics you don't want to discuss," she explained. "When a politician doesn't want to talk, it means he has something to hide."

"When a politician wants to talk," I responded, "it also means he has something to hide."

"So is your diet something you need to hide?"

The waitress stopped by the table and asked if we needed anything. Karla had her coffee topped off. I was still eyeballing my Perrier. Contrary to myth, vampires can and do drink water. Compared to blood, however, it's almost unbearably insipid.

"How about you, honey?" the waitress asked me. "You sure you don't want something to eat?"

"Not tonight, thanks."

Karla had a curious expression on her face as she watched the waitress. When the woman walked away, I asked what she'd been looking at.

"Her smile is a little bit like yours."

Again, I waited for an explanation.

"It's a nice smile," she said. "You just don't, you know,

open your mouth. You don't show your teeth. Are your teeth crooked, or something?"

"Not at all," I said. "In fact, they're perfect."

For some reason, this seemed to be of genuine interest to Karla. "Perfect? Really? Can I see?"

"No offense, Karla, but examining one another's orifices is somewhat outside the scope of our relationship."

She stopped chewing and glared at me. It seemed like a good time to change the subject.

"There's something I want to talk to you about," I said.

She started chewing again, but slowly.

"About a year ago, an off-duty Sacramento cop got killed in a motel down in Vacaville. You may not have heard about it. A guy named Dean Arnaud was shot in the head, executed. There were some unanswered questions about what he was doing at the motel. It looked like he was involved in something drug related, but it's possible he was looking for his missing niece. Either way, the police never caught the killer."

"Sorry," she said, "I don't pay much attention to the news."

"Anyway," I continued, "the guy's wife, Francine, was sure her husband was not involved in anything illegal. I guess she couldn't convince anyone else of his innocence. She eventually hired a private detective to try to clear Dean's name. Apparently, that didn't pan out, either, and the matter seems to have died there."

I put my index finger in the Perrier glass and stirred the ice around, then licked the water off my finger. Water, by any other name...

"So, what does all this have to do with anything?" Karla

asked.

"I'd like to find out if the P.I. knew anything about why Dean was in that motel in Vacaville."

"Why don't you ask the wife?"

"I would, but she isn't talking."

"Why not?" she asked. "Is she scared?"

"It's more intractable than that," I explained. "She's dead. She killed herself a few weeks ago."

"Shit! Was she, like, a friend of yours, or something?"

"No, I barely knew her. But I have some reasons of my own for wanting to know why her husband was killed."

Karla sipped her coffee and thought about it. "Couldn't you talk to the private eye?"

"I could, but I doubt if he'd tell me much. You know, client confidentiality, that sort of thing."

"So," she asked, anticipating where the conversation was leading, "is that where I come in?"

"If you're willing."

"What makes you think he'll talk to me?"

"He may not," I said. "On the other hand, he's male, divorced, probably lonely."

Karla grinned impishly, a mischievous sparkle in her eye. "You could break into his office and read his files."

"I already did that," I said flatly.

Her grin widened. "You broke into his office? Really?"

"His house, actually. He has an office in a spare bedroom."

Karla stared, her smile still spread across her face. She leaned forward, as if suddenly our conversation required more privacy. "You really did? You really broke into his house?"

"Does that surprise you?"

She sat back, crossed her arms and looked at me, her head cocked quizzically. "I hope you don't expect me to jump in the sack with this guy?"

I was weighing how to answer her when she apparently decided for herself that either I wasn't asking her to do that, or if I was asking, she was willing.

"What do you want me to do?" she asked.

"Go to this bar he frequents. Make yourself available for a little friendly conversation. If he obliges, see if you can get him to talk about the Arnauds. Maybe he'll tell you something that wasn't in his files."

"See if I can get him to talk about the Arnauds?" she asked, skeptically. "Should I just ask him, or am I supposed to somehow innocently steer the conversation to that one particular topic? I mean, the guy's probably had a lot of cases. Why should he suddenly start talking about that one?"

"I think it's better if you don't arouse his suspicion. I imagine you'll have to do some steering. For all I know, he may have forgotten about the Arnauds. On the other hand, there's always the possibility that the case still eats at him. Sometimes our failures stay with us more tenaciously than our successes. The Arnaud case could be stuck in his little private-eye brainpan, scratching at his professional self-image. Maybe a couple of drinks and a pretty face will loosen him up."

Karla picked quietly at her salad for several minutes. "You say this Arnaud guy was killed about a year ago?"

"About a year, yes."

Again, she sat quietly for several minutes. When she spoke, it was as though she'd figured something out and this had given her the resolve she was looking for. "I'll get him to talk."

•

On the following Tuesday, Karla picked me up at the footbridge at 7:30 p.m. She was wearing running shoes with cutoff jeans over black tights and a white blouse under her leather jacket. She'd replaced the spiked hair with a softer style, her makeup was more corporate, and her perfume had been applied more liberally.

"Evening, Shake."

"Bergamot and coriander." I said.

"Sorry?"

"Your perfume," I said. "Bergamot and coriander."

She'd started to pull away from the curb, but stopped, gawking at me like I'd just guessed some dark secret. "That's one hell of a nose you've got! Anything else you'd like to comment on? My bathing habits? Menstrual cycle?"

Those were things I could have commented on, but didn't. "Bergamot and coriander are both fairly distinctive fragrances. I wasn't complaining. I imagine Hamilton will like it, too."

She gave me a questioning look, then went back to her driving.

"Speaking of Hamilton," I said, "let's drive by The Intermission and see if his car is there. If it is, you can park across the street and I'll wait in the car while you do your stuff."

"Do my stuff?"

"Initiate a surreptitious attempt to extract information

122

from an unwitting subject."

"Right, do my stuff."

Karla was watching something in the rear view mirror. She let up on the gas, allowing the car to gradually slow. A moment latter, an SUV accelerated past us.

"I hate it when people tailgate. If he wants to stick his nose up someone's ass, why doesn't he go home and stick it up his wife's?"

"Feeling a little prickly tonight?" I asked.

"Sorry. I guess I'm a little nervous."

"Relax, Karla. You'll be fine. Nothing is riding on this. If Hamilton talks to you about Arnaud, good. If not, it doesn't matter. Either way, don't sweat it."

As it turned out, Hamilton's silver Volkswagen was in the parking lot. We parked in front of a Chinese restaurant across the street and I watched as Karla crossed the intersection and entered the bar. I reclined my seat so that I could just see the passing traffic above the dashboard, making myself comfortable for the wait. Even though it wasn't late, not yet even eight o'clock, there were very few pedestrians in the area. After a few minutes, two young girls passed on the sidewalk, a rapid-fire exchange of empty chatter pulling them on their way. "It was so, like, shut up!" one of them said. "She's like, in a bad mood. I'm like, okay!" the other said. I lost interest in them so quickly, it made me wonder if my attention span was even shorter than theirs.

A few minutes later, a sheriff's patrol car stopped in the turn lane at the intersection, then shot off against the light, tires smoking. When the car got up over the speed limit, its roof lights began flashing and the siren came on. I thought about some of the encounters I'd had over the years with the police. Most cops today, especially the young ones, are little more than punks with guns. I wonder sometimes if it's because they're the first generation of police to be brought up on video games and high-tech movies. If I didn't know better, I'd swear they all took their police academy training at Universal Studios. They definitely know how to talk the talk, but too often they aren't smart and they don't inspire confidence. And when the chips are down, it's not unusual for them to either piss themselves or go off half-cocked. I confess, I've put one or two out of their misery.

The night grew cooler and darker, the air slightly damp and very still. The minutes passed. The traffic gradually decreased. It was a little after ten o'clock when Karla came out of the bar. She crossed the street against the red light. There was a noticeable veering in her trajectory. She opened the driver's door and got in without her usual grace, plopping onto the seat, relieved to be free of the need to balance. After closing the door, she leaned her head back against the headrest and took several deep breaths before speaking.

"That was weird," she said. After a couple of minutes, she leaned her head forward and ran her fingers through her hair, then slapped her cheeks lightly as if trying to wake up. "Tell you what, Shake. That guy likes to talk."

"You okay? You're not going to puke, are you?"

"I'm fine. I never throw up from booze."

It sounded like one of those things people like to say about themselves, regardless of the facts, but I had no reason not to believe her.

"It was weird," she said again. "Like he was waiting for someone to talk to about Francine Arnaud. I go in, right? He's sitting at the bar, so I sit two stools over. I don't want to be too obvious. He looks like he's already had a few. So I order a beer and when it comes, I glance over. He's looking at me, so I tip my glass at him, just to be friendly, and he immediately moves over one stool and introduces himself. We do the small talk for a few minutes, he asks me what I do, do I like Sacramento, this and that. I make up some shit for answers. Then I ask him what he does. He says he's a private investigator. I'm duly impressed and after some more chitchat I ask him what was the most difficult or interesting case he ever worked on."

"Let me guess," I said. "Arnaud?"

"Arnaud. He tells me the whole story, from day one."

"So much for client confidentiality."

"Really! But here's the thing. He's not telling me all this because the case was interesting. He's telling me because he has a broken heart. The guy was in love with the Arnaud woman. I think it really tore him up that he couldn't help her, and then, to top it off, she committed suicide."

"The love angle is interesting, Karla, but I don't think it will help much."

"Yeah, I know," she agreed. "It doesn't explain anything except why he'd tell the whole story to a stranger in a bar."

"Did he say why Arnaud went to Vacaville?"

"He doesn't know. Couldn't ever get any solid answers. He knows Arnaud met someone at the motel, but he doesn't know who, or if it was about drugs or the niece, or both. He doesn't know if Arnaud was killed over the drugs or the niece, or over something else entirely. The only thing he seemed fairly sure of was that he didn't think there was any connection between Dean's drug activities and the missing girl. The niece had been gone a long time. Apparently, Dean didn't want to look for her but Francine pressured him into it."

"So he knows Arnaud was dirty?" I asked.

"Yeah. I guess everyone knew but the wife. Hamilton thinks telling Francine about her husband selling drugs was, as he put it, the worst mistake of his professional career. He thinks that's why she killed herself."

"Did he say anything about a guy named Richardson?"

"Richardson? Yeah, he thinks Richardson is some kind of big drug dealer, or something. He said he tried to talk to him, but Richardson wouldn't see him."

"Did he say why he wanted to talk to Richardson? What's the connection?"

"He doesn't know. He said Arnaud told his wife he was working on something, a possible connection to Richardson, but he didn't tell her what it was. He said he didn't want her to get her hopes up. Hamilton thinks it's entirely possible that Dean invented the connection to Richardson, just to make his wife think he was making progress."

"So he thinks Richardson didn't have anything to do with the murder?"

"He said it was a possibility, but he just didn't know. It's kind of sad, really. He thinks Francine would still be alive if he could have solved the murder."

For all of Hamilton's talking, I still didn't know whether Arnaud had gotten himself killed over drugs, or if it had something to do with the missing niece. No doubt, Richardson would have preferred the killing to be about something unrelated to his drug business. Denying the drug connection and shifting suspicion onto the missing girl might just have been an attempt to steer me away. But I had a hunch the niece was in the middle of it. As full of shit as Richardson was, he could very well have been right about the weakness of a drug-related motive. There wasn't that much money involved to risk killing a cop. But if Arnaud was killed because of the missing girl, that meant he'd dug deep enough to make someone very nervous.

"What about the niece?" I asked. "Did Hamilton try to find her?"

"He said he looked for her for a while, on his own, but drew a complete blank. He brags about how good he is at finding people, but the niece just vanished."

We sat quietly for a few minutes while I thought it over. Karla was starting to fidget. "How are you feeling? Sober enough to drive?"

"Yeah, and I need to pee."

She started the car and headed back. She did seem to have sobered up. At least she wasn't having any trouble driving. When we got to the footbridge, she pulled over to let me out.

"Are you going to look for the girl, Shake?"

"You did well tonight, Karla. I appreciate your help."

I stepped out and closed the door and Karla pulled away, smiling.

13

─────

For a vampire looking for a little distraction, the Arnaud mystery was an interesting puzzle: a wife deeply deceived about her husband's character, a husband who has given someone a reason to kill him, a missing girl, a possible drug connection. And as I pursued the puzzle, something else was adding to my curiosity; a familiar pattern, one that seemed to grow inevitably out of my entanglements with humans. As long as I kept my distance from human affairs, it wasn't particularly difficult to maintain caution in my day-to-day quest for blood. The less I had to do with people, the easier it was to avoid complications that might arise from killing them. But as soon as I stuck my nose into something unrelated to my basic nutritional needs, things had a tendency to get a little chaotic.

The problem was that involvement in people's affairs almost always presented me with unforeseen dining opportunities. It wasn't a question of being impulsive or reckless. The opportunities—more or less risky under the given circumstances—were simply there. I could either ignore them or take advantage of them, based on whatever concerns were relevant. I just had to use a little common sense in assessing the risk. Nevertheless, these improvised meals forced me to confront the fact that my decisions about who to kill, insofar as those decisions were the result of conscious evaluation, weren't based on much of anything beyond risk assessment and resource management.

However, there were exceptions. Every now and then, I

would chose not to kill someone, regardless of how low the risk was. There were people I judged to be worth more than a meal. Not just obvious cases, like Karla, who worked for me and was therefore worth more to me alive. Sometimes a complete stranger would do or say something, behave in a certain way, and I would unconsciously give them a pass. Which meant there were considerations that took precedence over my personal dietary needs. Which meant in turn that the forces and motivations of my own life were not entirely reducible to blood. It bothered me that I didn't understand how I was making these choices.

The Arnaud business was typical. I was curious about how the pieces fit together, but pursuing it had quickly led to two random meals: Richardson's girlfriend and Danny Weiss. There was something disconcertingly heedless about my actions. As if I were driven by forces I had no sway over. As if I had been reduced to physical processes, unable to weigh and evaluate the circumstances of my life. Because I wanted something from Richardson, I let the scumbag live, but drank his girlfriend's blood, as if her life and death were inconsequential. As if she didn't weigh in the balance of things. Then, with Danny Weiss, I did the opposite. I killed the little weasel and let the girl live. Danny may not have deserved any better, but it didn't change the fact that, beyond the physical satisfaction of my thirst, my motivations were unclear to me.

The truth was, I wanted there to be meaningful distinctions, points of reference. I wanted it to be possible to make a better or worse choice, so that I could make the better choice. But I didn't know how to make the distinctions. Consequently, killing often left me with the nagging uneasiness

129

of not knowing if I had made a mistake. Not necessarily an ethical mistake, but some kind of mistake; the kind you make when you do something irrevocable, knowing as you do it that you're taking a great deal for granted about something you really don't understand. The kind of mistake that reduces you to something less than you want to be.

For reasons that also weren't clear to me, unplanned meals seemed to bring all these unresolved questions to the surface, in a way that my routine feeding did not. There wasn't any logical explanation for it. Why would a planned killing like Francine's be any less unsettling? And that, too, was irritating. There was some kind of rationalization process at work that I wasn't comfortable with. Like a man who tells himself his actions are acceptable if he abides by the rules, keeps his goal in mind, and doesn't allow his greed to take precedence over his higher objectives. All the while, conveniently forgetting the possibility that the rules are only there in the first place to serve his greed.

14

Meandering through the aisles at the bookstore in the Pavilion Shopping Plaza, it occurred to me that there was a time, not so long ago, when you could walk into a bookstore and be fairly confident that it was staffed by bibliophiles. They might be eccentric, and probably were, but their eccentricities were tempered by a genuine affection for books. Today, most of the few surviving bookstores are corporate chains. They're run according to corporate policy, the employees are selected for their expendability, and with all the decor and the cafés, they're just extensions of the shopping mall concept.

The arrangement of books on the shelves has also undergone some curious modernizations. There often isn't any obvious relation between content and shelf location. I suspect categorization is the result of some kind of management excretion via marketing statistics. Not surprisingly, these market-driven arcana are as incomprehensible to the average employee as they are to shoppers. Staff people are reduced to performing their various tasks according to their own more or less illiterate whimsy. Add to that the typical American's regimen of daily pharmaceuticals, and you have a kind of stress-free commercial utopia where the staff is chemically indifferent to everything, including alphabetical order.

I was watching a young woman who had staked out one of the armchairs. The night wasn't particularly cold, but she was dressed for a winter assent of Denali. Her long coat, scarf, gloves, and hat were piled on the floor next to her chair, leaving what looked like no more than three or four layers of clothing to protect her from the elements inside the store. And I thought I was cold-blooded.

She had gathered a couple dozen books in a pile at her feet and was busying herself sorting through them. She would take the top book, flip nervously through the pages, then stuff it between the chair arm and either her left or right thigh. This process continued until she had sorted the entire pile, at which point she stood up and the two stacks of sorted books collapsed together into the space her butt had vacated. She put her coat on top of the books, tucked her cell phone into one of the coat pockets, and went to the restroom. I walked past the chair and deftly lifted the cell phone. There wasn't any necessity behind this. It wasn't as if the feds were tapping my home phone, or trying to triangulate on my location. It was more of a game whose practical implications, if there were any, were mostly just hypothetical. In the last few years, I'd been giving more thought to my technological footprint, the various ways of leaving digital crumbs along the trail of my misdeeds. Later that night I used the woman's phone to call Richardson.

"Goddamnit, Lisa," he barked into the phone, "I'm not paying for it!"

I'd obviously caught him in the middle of some delicate negotiations. "Hello, Ron. Having Lisa problems?"

The line was silent for several seconds. "It's you," he said, sounding relieved that I wasn't Lisa. "What do you want?"

"Thoughtful of you to ask, Ron. Especially after all your bullshit about not knowing Arnaud."

"Jesus! You're worse than the fucking cops."

"I haven't quite made up my mind whether to punish you

132

for lying to me, Ron, or give you an incentive to be more forthcoming."

There was another long silence. "You killed Danny Weiss, didn't you?"

"I read about that. A tragedy."

"Look, I admit I knew Arnaud. But I don't know why he was killed and I don't know who did it."

"Danny said something about a couple of Russians."

"Yeah? So?"

"Give me something useful and I'll let you keep your ten thousand dollars for November."

I could almost hear his mental cash register ringing. "I don't know, maybe I can find something. Let me get this straight. If I do this, I don't have to pay you anymore?"

"Not quite, Ron. You don't have to pay me for November."

"How about November and December?"

The guy was too much. "I'll tell you what. You give me something I can use, we'll cancel the November payment. Depending on how things progress from there, I'll consider canceling December, too."

"All right," he said, after a long pause. "I'll see what I can dig up. How can I get in touch with you?"

"Don't try to be clever. I'll call you again on Wednesday evening. That gives you five days. If you can't come up with anything, you'll still have time to make your November deposit. And Ron, don't waste my time."

"Anyone ever tell you you're an asshole?"

"I'm a lot worse than that. I'll talk to you on Wednesday, and good luck with Lisa."

I removed the SIM card from the phone and tossed everything into the trash, then booted the computer to check my email. Along with the usual spam, there was a note from Mio saying she was going to be in Sacramento on business for a few days in early December, and she was looking forward to seeing me. There was a P.S. informing me that I would be required to take her out dancing at least one evening. This was partly a way of teasing me. She knew I didn't like the club scene, or dancing, for that matter, but I nevertheless had an obligation to meet her "at least one evening" minimum. Dancing was one of her passions, along with making money and martial arts, and she was extraordinarily talented at all three.

I had little more than a vague impression of the overall scope of Mio's finances. I never asked her for specifics, mainly because I wasn't particularly interested. Money was a topic that quickly bored me. I knew she was wealthy. She had investments all over the world: in digital technologies, in oil and natural gas, in biotech and pharmaceuticals. These were things she'd mentioned in the past, before she realized the true extent of my indifference and stopped talking about it. I also knew that, in addition to the Sacramento house she put at my disposal, she owned other properties in California, as well as in Florida, Quebec, Paris, in several East European and Central Asian countries, and in Japan.

On the other hand, I was rather fascinated by Mio's interest in martial arts. I knew it had little, if anything, to do with acquiring the skill to defend herself. She was a vampire. With her vampire's strength and speed, there was no need for her to train. It was the "art" of martial arts that she was drawn to, expressed primarily in dance. The various martial arts styles are sometimes divided into two general groups: the hard, fighting styles, and what are sometimes disparagingly referred to as the soft, dancing styles. With Mio, the distinction evaporated. She developed her own techniques, mixing hard and soft elements, incorporating all of it into dance. And if there was ever a dance of death, Mio was its ultimate practitioner.

At the same time, she was thoroughly pragmatic. Aesthetics aside, if martial arts didn't offer her practical advantages, I don't think she would have bothered. One important advantage her skills gave her was a way to disguise, at least partially, her vampire powers. Whenever possible, human beings will interpret strange, anomalous, or outlandish events in a way that minimizes the strain on their expectations. If people happen to witness Mio's astonishing physical prowess, it's much easier for them to incorporate what they see if they think of it in terms of something familiar, like martial arts. By stylizing her actions, she can predispose witnesses to interpretations that explain away her otherwise implausible abilities.

Mio and I have talked about it on occasion. The Matrix trilogy, the Blade trilogy, the modern Chinese kung fu fantasies full of flying monks tip-toeing across tree tops, all the super-heroes from the comic books adapted to the screen via computerized special effects technology. After a couple of decades of this kind of visual experience, people today seem almost eager to witness in real life the fantasies they've seen so often on the screen. The line between the possible and the impossible, between credibility and incredibility, has shifted slightly in a way that can be made to work to Mio's advantage. With a touch of the theatrical, she can get away with things that in the past would have jarred people's sense of reality. She was a true artist at this kind of perceptual subterfuge.

Myself, I tended not to bother. In this respect, Mio and I were exact opposites. She adapted to the human milieu by immersing herself in human affairs, using their social dynamics to her own advantage. Her interest in martial arts was a good example of this. But I didn't work that way. I preferred to minimize my need to adapt by having as little as possible to do with people. Where Mio might be conspicuous, even theatrical, I did my best to blend in. Mio could perform in public, artfully nudging witnesses toward interpretations that squared with their imaginations. I found it much simpler to avoid public performance. Maybe I just wasn't subtle enough. Or maybe I knew, intuitively, that the safest place for me was outside of the human imagination.

15

I called Richardson the following Wednesday from a pay phone in the university library.

"What have you got for me, Ron?"

"I want to make something clear first," he said. "I didn't have anything to do with killing that cop. All I did was set up a buy."

"For the Russians Danny mentioned?"

"Danny was full of shit."

"Meaning?"

"I set up the buy for Arnaud but I didn't tell Danny anything about any Russians. Or anything the fuck else, for that matter."

"Maybe Arnaud told him."

"Arnaud was definitely stupid enough. But it didn't happen. He didn't know who the customer was, and neither did Danny. I told Arnaud where and when to meet the buyer. That's it. The Russians were Danny's bullshit."

"He said you mentioned the Russians being in town for a Kings game."

"That's bullshit! You could ask the little prick, but... oh yeah, you killed him. So I guess you'll have to take my word for it."

"If you keep lying to me, Ron, I'm going to take a lot more than your word."

"Goddamnit! I'm not lying."

"If neither of them knew who the buyer was, why did

Danny say it was two Russians, one with a 404 tattoo on his hand? That's a fairly specific description of someone he didn't know."

After a protracted silence, I asked, "Who was buying the dope from Arnaud?"

After another protracted silence, Richardson said, "That's the funny part."

"Amuse me, Ron."

"I don't know where the fuck you're going with this, but wherever it is, you've got to leave my name out of it."

"Talk, Ron."

"It was for a guy named Stephen Yavorsky. He's not Russian, he's Ukrainian."

"This isn't helping your credibility."

"Look, I don't know why Danny told you about Russians. The little prick. Knowing you, he was probably scared shitless and told you the first thing that came into his head."

"So, who's Yavorsky?" I asked.

"He lives in San Francisco. I don't know that much about him. He likes to party. He sends his guys up to Sac now and then to buy coke from Danny. Or he used to."

"So why'd you hook him up with Arnaud instead of Danny? Why drag a dirty cop into the picture?"

"That was Yavorsky's idea."

"He asked you to set up the buy specifically from Arnaud?"

"Yeah. I know it sounds suspicious. I asked him what the fuck was going on. He said some shit about wanting the connection to the cops. The guy's a little weird. He thinks he's still in the fucking Ukraine, or something."

138

"Sounds like Arnaud was being set up, wouldn't you say?"

"Yeah, so?"

"You don't know why?" I asked.

"No fucking idea."

Richardson was only telling me enough to make his story plausible. For the time being, anyway, I agreed that he had earned a reprieve on his November deposit.

Later that night, I did some research on Stephen Yavorsky. The guy made a lot of money in the early 90s, after the breakup of the Soviet Union. He was well positioned to benefit from Ukraine's independence, and sufficiently independent himself to leave his homeland as soon as his newly-acquired wealth made it possible. He landed in San Francisco in 1996, made a few solid investments and blended into the Bay Area business community. Among other things, he owned a nightclub in North Beach called Satellite. That was the surface picture. His extra-legal activities, whatever they were, apparently required muscle on his payroll. Still, there was a big difference between recreational drug use and murder. And none of it explained how the missing niece was involved, if in fact she was.

There were a number of ways I could pursue it, but since Mio would be in town soon, I decided to wait until she arrived. I was going to have to take her dancing anyway, and Yavorsky's club was as good a place as any. There was no reason to think dropping into Satellite would tell me anything about Dean Arnaud, but I might learn something useful about Yavorsky.

•

I called Karla the next day and asked her to meet me at the footbridge at 9:00 p.m. It was November 30th, payday. She was waiting when I arrived. I got in the car and closed the door. "Good evening, Karla."

She was wearing jeans and a t-shirt, tennis shoes and her black leather jacket. "Good evening, Shake."

I handed her a manila envelope. "It's payday."

She smiled and took the envelope. "Are we going somewhere?"

"Not tonight. I just wanted to pay you for November."

She opened the envelope and looked inside, then at me. "It looks like a lot."

"Twelve thousand dollars. Five thousand is your base salary for November. There's five hundred for driving me to Richardson's on the first, five hundred for taking me to the movie on the sixteenth, a thousand for talking to Hamilton on the twenty-first. That's seven thousand. The other five thousand is for that little episode out in Sloughhouse on the sixth. Is that acceptable?"

She held the envelope open in her lap, staring at the money inside. "You're paying me an extra five thousand dollars for fucking up? I was afraid you were going to fire me."

"It's not for fucking up," I said. "It's for coping with a difficult situation."

"I don't think I coped all that well," she said, with obvious sincerity. "If it wasn't for you, I'd probably still be there, in the bushes somewhere, dead."

"You were only there in the first place because I had you take me there. The thought of firing you never crossed my mind.

In fact, I was worried you might quit."

She was still staring into the envelope.

"You thought about quitting, didn't you?" I asked.

"I thought about it," she admitted. "I think if you would have let that guy walk away, I would have quit. I know there are lots of guys like him in the world. I mean, I know they're out there. I'm not naive. But if he'd walked away, there wouldn't have been anything to balance out the fear. Does that make any sense?"

"I think I understand. And that's why I want to pay you. For your courage. Not so much the courage you showed facing some vicious shit who got pleasure out of hurting people. That wasn't the main thing."

She looked at me questioningly. "It wasn't?"

"No, the main thing was the courage you showed in coping with what I did to him. That may sound odd to you, but I appreciate the fact that you didn't lose your grip, or come back later and ask me to justify what I'd done. For that, I have no problem paying you."

Karla folded the envelope and stuck it in her jacket pocket.

"By the way," I said, "do you remember when you picked up the car from Tony's garage and he mentioned a friend of mine named Mio?"

"Yeah, I remember asking you if she was your wife and you didn't answer."

"She's not my wife. Just a friend. She's going to be in Sacramento for a few days, sometime in the next week or so. I was wondering if you like to dance?"

"Yes," she said, tentatively. "I love dancing."

"That's good. So does Mio. If you don't mind, I'd like you

141

to go out with us one night. We'll probably drive down to San Francisco."

"Okay. I take it I'm not going just as the driver?"

"Correct. I'm not much of a dancer. I was hoping you could provide some company for Mio. She may invite Tony, too. If so, he'll also be glad you came. He's rather shy and he gets a lot of startled attention on a dance floor, surrounded by regular-sized people."

Karla laughed. "Isn't Tony married?"

"Yes, happily. His relationship with Mio is strictly business."

"I thought he was a mechanic."

I wasn't sure how much of Tony's relationship with Mio I wanted to discuss. There wasn't anything secret about it. I simply preferred to let them both do their own PR work. "He is a mechanic. You can ask them about it yourself, if you're interested."

I also wasn't sure if I should try to somehow prepare Karla for meeting Mio. Of course, there wasn't any way to do that. With Mio, it was always trial by fire. I decided there wasn't any point.

"I'm not sure yet what Mio's plans are, but I'll be in touch."

———

16

Mio arrived the following Thursday, about an hour before dawn. I was in the shoebox reading *Extinction*, a novel by Thomas Bernhard, when I heard a noise coming from my office. I'd been surfing some history sites earlier and my computer was still on, so I woke it up and clicked the icon that opened the office surveillance camera. Mio was standing next to the desk, removing her earrings. The lights in the office had been off earlier, but now the desk lamp was on. This provided enough light for the camera, which, as the next couple of minutes left no doubt, was the reason she'd turned on the lamp. She knew I would be watching.

She dropped her earrings into her handbag lying on the desk, then proceeded to remove several long pointed needles, about the size of chopsticks, from the mass of hair collected in a bun at the back of her head. With each needle the bun became less compact, finally falling in a thick black wave that reached below mid-thigh. She unbuttoned her blouse, took it off, folded it neatly and laid it on the desk, then did the same with her skirt. I had never known Mio to wear a bra. She paused briefly, as if considering, then lowered her panties until they fell to the floor. Her pubic hair was thick, luxurious and black as night. She scratched it vigorously, fluffing up the matted hair, then stepped gracefully out of her shoes and walked toward the secret panel leading to the shoebox.

At this point, I was as beside myself as a vampire is likely to get. I dashed back to my lounge chair and picked up the novel, pretending to be absorbed. When the panel slid open and Mio stepped through, I looked up in mock surprise, using the book to conceal the bulge in my pants. No matter how precise my memory of Mio might be, it always failed to prepare me for seeing her in the flesh. Mio's face was not, in any conventional sense, beautiful. She had what might be described as a horse face: long and narrow, with a high forehead, a long, broad, flat nose, and a wide mouth with narrow lips. She also had very pronounced epicanthic folds and extraordinarily narrow slits for eyes. Nevertheless, these features somehow managed to harmonize with the most unexpected charm.

Just under five feet tall and an eternal ninety-one pounds, she was an incarnation of feminine animal vitality: slender, narrow-hipped, densely muscular, but without any suggestion of either adolescence or masculinity. Her body exuded a formidable prowess, tangible in predators like leopards and other big cats, but rare in a creature possessing self-consciousness. Her simple presence could be deeply unsettling, even for another vampire. Especially for another vampire. She was, in her own way, magnificently beautiful. However, saying this did not convey anything fundamental. It only concealed something much more profound. There was something about her: a force, an energy, something spooky and invisible, like radiation, that burned into everything around her.

I first met Mio in Mexico in 1976. Many parts of the country were in a state of civil unrest, and I was there taking advantage of the chaotic conditions, using them to mask my feeding on humans. By that time in my life as a vampire, I was very much a loner, having given up any wish to associate with others of my kind. So I was not all that pleased to be interrupted one evening by another vampire. In truth, we were both initially put off by the presence of the other, but we were both also curious, intrigued by the improbability of our encounter. As the night passed, we found ourselves unexpectedly comfortable together. The novelty made us careless and we lost track of the time. As dawn approached, we realized we would have to push ourselves in order to make it back to my lodging, which was closer than hers, before the sun put an unpleasant end to the evening.

If you've ever watched a world-class sprinter compete, you may be able to imagine the driving intensity required to propel a two-legged animal at forty-plus miles per hour. Then consider that I'm a head taller than Mio and for every two strides of mine, she had to take three to keep up. But she did keep up. She was like some incredible machine driven by her own velocity. Her arms and legs churned in a blur of absolute and precise physical determination. With a few hundred yards to go, the sun was starting to peak above the horizon. The threat of death along with the all-out exertion to reach cover, produced in me a kind of euphoria. I would have laughed if I'd had any breath to spare. It was then that I witnessed something I did not expect. Mio began to pull ahead of me. With all my strength, I could not keep up with her. Witnessing her under those extreme conditions, seeing her terrifying will to survive manifest itself in the physical perfection of her body pushed to its absolute limit, was for me the single most pure and intense moment of beauty I have ever experienced.

We reached my lodgings with only seconds to spare. Once safely inside, it was all I could do to breathe. When my heart finally stopped pounding, I realized Mio was crouching naked across the room, watching me silently through the narrow slits of her eyes. That was to be the first time I would have sex since 1908. It was also the first of many times I would witness the gymnastic precision Mio was capable of. She sprang across the room like she'd been shot from a cannon and hit me chest to chest. Her legs locked around my waist, she wrapped her left arm around my neck and pressed her mouth hard against mine, while simultaneously her right hand had unzipped my fly and grasped my cock. I felt myself swell in her hand as she guided me into her.

She stopped kissing me long enough to say the only words she would speak for some time. "Don't do anything. Just stand still."

She pressed her mouth back to mine and began slowly raising and lowering herself on me. I stood obediently, my back braced against the wall, amazed once again by what it meant to be a vampire.

And now, in the quiet of the shoebox, Mio stood before me again, naked, her expression betraying no emotion. I moved the book aside and let it fall to the floor, unbuckled my belt, unfastened and unzipped my pants, raised myself enough to push my pants down below my knees, then relaxed back into the lounge chair. I had not seen Mio for almost six months, an absence made unmistakably salient by my erection. Mio stood as if frozen for an eternity that must have lasted two or three minutes. Almost clinically, she reached between her legs and slipped a finger into her vagina. Without looking at her hand, she let it fall back to her side, rubbing the moisture between finger and thumb. Apparently satisfied, she walked forward, climbed into the chair, her knees straddling my hips, and once again guided me inside her.

●

Later in the day, after we'd slept, I told Mio about Arnaud; everything from the night I drank Francine's blood to the information I'd gotten from Richardson about Yavorsky.

"And all of this," Mio asked, stretched out on the bed, "because the word 'bloodsucker' was printed on a photograph in a trunk in a dead woman's closet?"

"Well, no. It's a little more complicated than that." I said. "For one thing, it wasn't just any photograph, but one of a man I already had a certain interest in. It wasn't just the word 'bloodsucker.' That was just a detail that initially caught my attention."

"Okay. I can see how you might have been intrigued by the photo popping up in the dead woman's closet. I don't share your fascination with coincidence, but that's me. The photo reminded you of your previous interest in Richardson and then you decided to go after him for financial reasons. Fine. What I don't get is what any of this has to do with Arnaud's murder, or why you would care about that."

"There may not be any connection, and I don't pretend to care who killed Dean Arnaud, or why. I'm just curious about how it all fits together, if in fact it does fit together. Most likely, nothing will come of it. I'll have wasted a little time. On the other hand, life is full of surprises. And it's not like I don't have the spare time."

Mio signed audibly.

"What?" I asked.

"It's so like you, Shake. For all of your plans and schedules and precautions and all the routines you structure your daily life around, it's adventure you're really after. You're like a wild animal sitting quietly in a room, patiently waiting for an excuse to leap out the window."

It was my turn to sigh. "Maybe you're right."

"I am right. It's one of the things I like about you. One of your most endearing qualities. We both know you're wearing a mask, and I like you just fine when you're wearing it. We also both know you have to take it off now and then, and that's when the fun begins."

"Then why do I get the impression you're trying to talk me out of something?"

"I'm not, Shake. I'm just expressing an opinion. I agree, the world is full of surprises. But the unexpected connections between mundane events are usually just as mundane as the events they connect. As they say, shit happens. It just seems to me that the life you've carved out for yourself here in suburbia is your way of not stepping in human shit. So I'm a little confused when you go off looking for something to step in."

"Aren't you the one who thinks I'm too domesticated?" I asked.

"For my tastes, Shake. What works for you is your business. And I'm not cautioning you about taking chances. I know you can take care of yourself and I know you could get along just fine without all these domestic props. I just don't understand why, if your stability is important to you, you would incur the risk. This Arnaud business seems like the perfect way

148

to stumble into a mess that will end up blowing your quiet life all to hell. The murder of a crooked cop, no less. Really, Shake, isn't this something you ought to avoid?"

"I don't think there's much risk involved."

Mio waved her hand impatiently. "Well, it's your time. You can fill it however you want. Personally, I think you'd be better off doing crossword puzzles. At least then you could improve your vocabulary."

It was unusual for Mio to be glib. Unless she simply wanted to change the subject. My expression must have betrayed my feelings.

"I'm not really serious, Shake," she said. "I know as well as you do that the world tends to surprise us in all kinds of ways. Who knows what little treasures you might find?"

"The world isn't just surprising, Mio. It's deeply mysterious. It may look to you like I'm chasing intangibles. And maybe I am. But either way, my curiosity is all I really have. If I stumble across some apparently chance convergence, like Richardson's photo in Francine's closet, I don't just assume there's a deeper significance, and then go chasing after it. At least not with the expectation of finding anything. But I can't let that stop me from looking."

"You like to chase coincidence?"

"I suppose I do. It allows me to act as if the world made sense. For me, coincidence is like a little peephole in a wall. I can pass by without looking and miss whatever might be on the other side. Or I can put my eye up to the hole and satisfy my curiosity. If I choose to look, I may not be able to see much. And most of the time it's as you say: trivial and mundane. But not always. And either way, the peephole gives me something to focus on."

"I understand, Shake. Really, I do. The world doesn't supply us with reasons to do anything other than drink blood. For everything else, we have to come up with our own reasons, our own incentives. I wasn't criticizing your choices. I just forget sometimes how different you and I are."

After several minutes, Mio said, "I know you've thought about this a lot, Shake. And regardless of what you may think, so have I. No matter how different we might be, we want the same thing. We want to feel like there is some meaning in what we do. I make money by beating humans at their own games. It entertains me, and at the same time, it provides me with effective and efficient strategies for acquiring what I need most from people: their blood. But in the end, the games are just games. I know there isn't any deeper meaning to them, no more than the coincidences you chase have some deeper meaning. You want to penetrate the world's mystery because you're alone and you think you might discover something that will reduce the pain of your solitude. And maybe you will. I don't know."

"Aren't you alone, too, Mio?"

"I am. But not like you. My life keeps me busy. It may only give me an illusion of purpose, but it's a comforting illusion. That doesn't seem to work for you. I wonder sometimes if absolute solitude isn't what you're really after."

Mio knew well enough why I lived such a solitary life. She had the same choices I had. Vampires can band together, create their own little communities, where people only enter the picture at mealtime. Most vampires attempt to live this way, attempt to find what solace they can in the relationships they cultivate with each other. But in the long run, it rarely works.

The so-called community is contrived, the relationships are forced, and the solace they provide isn't enough to hold it all together for long.

On the other hand, there are a few vampires who attempt to accomplish the same thing by aligning themselves with human society. They don't pretend to be human. Rather, they immerse themselves in human affairs, try to feed on human purpose at the same time they feed on human blood. But this strategy, too, almost never works. It requires too fine a balance between emotional involvement and ruthless detachment. The fundamental relationship of eater to eaten constantly upsets the balance. Mio was the only vampire I'd ever known who could maintain that balance for any length of time. I couldn't do it. It required an affinity for contradictions that I simply lacked.

The problem was really deeper than that. Everything a human being does is ultimately driven by mortality. The motivations that feed human ambition draw their energy from impending death. All the paraphernalia of human life—wanting a family, a career, success, fame, fortune, security, the longing to make something of themselves—all of it draws its urgency from the fact that death is just around the corner. Human civilization is a complex web of rationalizations, not only to aid survival, but also to create the illusion that there is some pressing reason why they ought to survive.

None of this computes for a vampire, for the simple reason that death is not around the corner, at least not on a human scale of time. The human agenda—get an education, choose a career, find a mate, make more little humans, work like a slave, retire, lapse into a second childhood, die—is an itinerary for a journey vampires don't take. As far as I was concerned, if I wasn't going

151

to take the journey, there wasn't any reason to carry the baggage.

All of which for me came down to a life of solitude, punctuated intermittently by brief periods of intimacy with Mio—the only vampire I'd met in a hundred years who offered even the slightest possibility of companionship. The others, if I'd had to associate with them on any regular basis, would have quickly driven me to take a short mid-afternoon stroll. But Mio and I were not emotionally dependent on one another. We were always conscious of moderating our involvement, knowing as we both did that our compatibility was inversely proportionate to the amount of time we spent in one another's company.

"Maybe you're right," Mio said. "Maybe you don't have a choice. Maybe solitude is the only realistic option for you."

"Solitude doesn't recommend itself to you because you actually like people," I said.

"So do you, sometimes. Your new driver, for instance. The way you talk about her, it's obvious you like her."

"I do like her," I admitted. "And that's a problem for me in a way that it wouldn't be a problem for you. You can socialize with humans, be with people you like, people whose company you enjoy. You can work with them, employ them, entertain and be entertained by them, and turn around and kill them at the drop of a hat. It's not easy for me to do that."

"So kill the ones you don't like. There are plenty of those, especially in your case."

I grew silent.

"Look, Shake, the big difference between us is that you think human beings should be divided into two groups: those whose lives are less important than your dinner, and those who, for some arbitrary reason of your own, deserve to be taken off the menu. I don't make that distinction. If I choose not to drink someone's blood today, that doesn't mean they won't be the *soup du jour* tomorrow. Either way, I really don't care about the reasons. Whatever they are, they're good enough for me. Because no matter what they are, they're my reasons. They're always my reasons. And that's what counts for me."

"I understand what you're saying, Mio, and it's not so much that I disagree with you. It's just that when I decide to let someone live, my reasons for doing so tend to take on a life of their own. I suppose because I want them to. I want the reasons to endure. I want the reasons to be there for me in the future."

Mio was giving me what I took to be a quizzical look, which, since her face rarely betrayed any emotion, consisted of tilting her head slightly to the side. "My dear Shake, you're thinking like a human. A hundred years from now, the people you've let live will all be long dead, and your reasons for having let them live will be forgotten. You however, will be just as you are now. Or very nearly so. Perhaps in another hundred years you will have given up your search for good humans."

"I know you don't agree," I said. "But some people deserve to be taken off the menu."

"If you say so, Shake. But I think that's your own self-interest talking. For some reason, you want there to be good humans. But what you aren't willing to admit is that what makes them good is your own interest. As I see it, the good human is one who has a diminished capacity to do me harm. But all that really means is that they are people of diminished capacity. Give them power and you'll see what their goodness is worth."

I didn't exactly disagree, but I couldn't get around the feeling that Mio's point of view was just too simplistic. The world isn't that black and white. As important as Mio was to me, I knew that her world was governed by self-interest because she was governed by self-interest. She wasn't burdened by the choices she made because everything else was secondary to her own needs and desires. Of course, according to her, I was the same. But even if she was right, even if we were the same, our interests were not the same. I knew this was why, as important as Mio was to me, she was not, nor would she ever be, enough. And if she was not enough, I doubted that any vampire ever would be. It was not a comforting thought.

17

We drove to San Francisco on Saturday. I wasn't ready to tell Karla where I lived, so Mio and I took a cab downtown to the Hyatt Regency on L Street. I'd given Karla a call on Friday instructing her to meet us in the lobby at 8:00 p.m. I'd also given her directions to Tony's house so she could pick him up on the way downtown.

During our cab ride, Mio showed me her new handbag. She asked me to examine it and see if I noticed anything unusual about it. It was small, only about eight by six inches, made of a very fine, soft leather. There was a long, thin strap, also leather, connected by jade rings at the two upper corners. The bag opened at the top by a clasping mechanism made of what looked like a high grade of burnished steel. The clasp consisted of four steel rings. At first, the four rings appeared to be a single piece, but on closer examination I saw there were two sections, one of three rings, the other of the remaining single ring. There wasn't anything novel about the mechanism itself, aside from its exceptional workmanship. By pressing in opposite directions, the fourth ring snapped briskly apart from the other three, allowing the bag to open.

The opening was straight and rigid, the two sections of steel spreading apart at each end by expanding accordion-like folds of leather. The inside consisted of a single compartment containing a small makeup kit, two keys on a key ring set with a very large emerald, a California driver's license giving Mio's age as twenty-three, and what looked like about three thousand dollars in hundreds in a money clip. I removed everything and placed it on the seat between us. The bag was lined with a patterned silk of exceptional quality and didn't appear to have any secret compartments. The only thing that struck me as curious was its weight; it was heavier than I expected it to be. The weight was all at the top, which, given the thickness of steel used in the clasp, was what one would expect.

I knew Mio had a reason for showing me the bag, and given enough time, I probably would have figured it out. But whatever I was supposed to be looking for was not obvious. I replaced the bag's contents and handed it back to her. She took it, casually sliding three fingers of her right hand into the three connected rings of the clasp. I heard a faint click and the bag dropped to her lap. Still in her hand was a very mean looking weapon, something like a combination knife and brass knuckles. Sized to fit Mio's fingers, the three rings served as a grip. What would otherwise have been the brass knuckles part was machined into a blade running the width of the rings. When attached to the bag, the weapon was cleverly concealed as part of the bag's construction. Being punched by someone wearing this on their hand would be like getting hit with a razor sharp axe.

"Taka-san made it for me," Mio said. "The workmanship is quite impressive, don't you think?"

Among other things, Taka-san was famous for his custom made knives. I only knew this because Mio had once shown me some of his creations. "Very impressive," I admitted. "Did he make the whole thing? The bag, too?"

"Everything. I gave him a Fendi handbag as a model, but he made this one from scratch. When it was finished, I had one of my gallery employees deliver it to me. I wanted her to carry it through airport security, to see if it aroused any suspicion. Of course, it didn't."

"So, who are you planning to cut?" I asked.

"No one in particular. The main reason I had him make it for me was so I could pay him. His daughter isn't healthy, and he's spent most of his money sending her to various clinics in the U.S. and Europe. I'd give him the money, but he's very proud. This way, he earns it. His fees are a bit extravagant, but in another twenty or thirty years, after he's been dead for a while, everything he's ever made will have increased in value many times. Commissioning the bag helps him now and it's a good investment for me."

I was sure these were practical considerations that weighed in her commissioning the bag, but it was obvious she had given Taka-san the assignment at least partly out of fondness. With Mio, it was difficult to know what the admixture might be. "He must be getting pretty old," I said.

"He's seventy-nine. He still has the hands of a brain surgeon, but his eyesight is going."

"What's wrong with his daughter?"

"Multiple sclerosis, for one. She's also an insufferable bitch, but I suppose that's beside the point."

•

Across the street from the state capital, the Hyatt looks like a committee-generated facsimile of post-modern Mediterranean

157

luxury. The cab dropped us in front of the lobby. We were about twenty minutes early, so Mio suggested we wait inside. We found a sofa not far from the front desk and took a seat. One of the staff, a young Asian woman, approached and asked if we would like a cup of coffee. I'd never been to the Hyatt before, so I didn't know if this level of hospitality was normal, or if it had something to do with Mio. It's often like that with her. She projects a presence that is almost regal. In the absence of any guiding etiquette, people have a tendency to become a bit servile around her. There was also the fact that her clothes and jewelry were easily worth more than the young woman's annual salary, a fact the woman was no doubt more sensitive to than I was.

Mio opened her purse and took out two one-hundred-dollar bills. "We're fine, we're just waiting for some friends." She held out the two hundreds when she said this. "I wonder if you could change these to twenties for me?"

The young woman took the money without a word and walked back to the front desk. When she returned, she counted out ten twenties and gave them to Mio. Mio separated one bill, deftly folding it into quarters with one hand and held it out to the woman as a tip. When the woman took the money, Mio gently squeezed her hand as she pressed the bill into her palm. The woman momentarily lost her professional composure, flushed a deep red, then mumbled a thank you and hurried away.

"What was that about?" I asked.

Mio dropped the twenties into her handbag and gave me a dismissive little shrug by way of telling me to mind my own business. A few minutes later, Tony walked through the sliding glass doors at the front entrance. Grandiose architecture, like courthouses and pretentious hotel lobbies, tend to dwarf the humans who inhabit them. This is what they're supposed to do. The courthouse is meant to intimidate, the hotel lobby to give the illusion of status by virtue of scale. The guy at the front desk did a double take when Tony walked in. He probably wasn't used to seeing someone big enough to diminish the lobby's pretensions.

Tony saw us sitting on the sofa and performed a minimalist gesture that consisted of raising one index finger, pointed in our direction, as if he were shooting from the hip. Mio waved back, more conspicuously, and stood up. Tony waited while we crossed the lobby. The two of them shook hands. The difference in size was like an adult shaking hands with a four year old, but they carried it off naturally enough, though Tony had a look of mild awe on his face. Mio was no doubt one of the few people other than Tony's wife, Patricia, who was seemingly indifferent to his physical dimensions.

"Good evening, Tony," Mio said.

"Good evening, Mio. You look dangerous tonight."

"Why, thank you. You're looking pretty good, yourself"

Tony shook my hand. "Shake."

"Tony, good to see you."

The three of us walked to the car. Mio said she'd sit in back. Tony opened the back door for her on the passenger side. I went around to the driver's side and got in behind Karla. It was the sensible arrangement, since Tony needed to put the seat all the way back in order to make room for his knees, whereas Mio needed no legroom at all. After slipping her shoes off, she sat with her legs curled under her on the seat.

When we were all in, Karla turned around and looked at

Mio. "Hi, I'm Karla Lambretti."

"Mio Nagaishi."

Mio looked at me, her expression a mixture of amused curiosity and playful reprimand, then turned her attention back to Karla. "Now that I've had a look at you," she said, "I can see Shake hasn't been entirely forthcoming. He told me you were attractive, but he didn't tell me you were stunning."

Karla smiled, her eyes fixed on Mio. "Shake hasn't told me much about you, either, except that you're not his wife and you like to dance."

"Two of the essentials," Mio said.

I wasn't particularly interested in seeing how long the two of them could keep this up. "It's a long drive to San Francisco. Why don't we talk on the road?"

The conversation lagged while Karla got us to the freeway heading west. Mio was leaning into the corner, her body angled toward Karla, studying her profile while she drove. Mio was showing a little more interest in Karla than I'd expected, but I assumed she'd tell me what was on her mind, if and when she chose. Tony sat quietly until Karla asked him a question.

"So, Tony, if you don't mind my asking, what do you do for Mio?"

Tony looked her way briefly, then returned his eyes to the road ahead. "I accompany her."

Karla waited patiently for an elaboration that didn't come. Mio finally offered one.

"Tony keeps the wolves off me."

"He's like a bodyguard?" Karla asked.

"Not exactly. More of a caution sign—to other men who think I might be grateful for their attention."

Karla and Tony exchanged looks. Apparently Tony didn't feel the need to add anything, so Mio continued.

"A woman as fine looking as you, Karla, knows what goes through the minds of men when they see you walk into a room. I'm not as beautiful as you are, but that doesn't stop men from thinking I'd make a nice little oriental sex toy. It gets so tiresome sometimes, like having a swarm of flies constantly buzzing around your face."

"I see," Karla said, "the flies see Tony and they think twice about doing anything that might get them swatted."

"It works pretty well, most of the time," Mio said.

Karla sized Tony up, as if she'd forgotten how big he was. "When it doesn't, does Tony rescue you?"

Mio considered the question. "Do you rescue me, Tony?"

Tony answered as if reciting from memory. "Under no circumstances do I intervene between Mio and any man, woman, child or animal that I judge to be a threat to her. No exceptions."

Karla was incredulous. "I don't get it. You don't help her if some jackass starts getting rough?"

"It's part of the deal," Tony said, "between the three of us: myself, my wife and Mio."

"Patricia doesn't want Tony getting into any trouble," Mio explained. "I pay him to accompany me, to be present, nothing more. Ninety-nine percent of the time, that's all I need. The other one percent I deal with myself."

Karla fell silent. I suspected she was thinking along the same general lines I was: Could Tony really resist stepping in to help the tiny little Mio? If so, it made me wonder just how much Tony knew about her. They'd had a working arrangement for several years. Maybe Tony had seen Mio in action and that was enough for him to accept the idea that she didn't need his help. Karla, on the other hand, had no idea what Mio was capable of, and their explanations were only confusing her.

Mio, sensing Karla's perplexity, changed the subject. "How long have you been working for Shake?"

"Just a few weeks."

"How's it working out? Is he treating you right?"

"All in all, it's going pretty well, I think."

"What were you doing before you started working for Shake?"

"Tending bar, mostly."

"Mostly? What else?"

Karla hesitated, glancing in the mirror before answering. "Well, actually, I was turning tricks. Not regular. Just now and then, for the extra cash."

Mio absorbed Karla's disclosure without the slightest indication of surprise. "That's risky, isn't it? You're not still doing that, are you?"

"No. Not since I started working for Shake."

"I'm glad to hear it. Shake should be paying you enough to leave all of that behind you."

"He is. Absolutely," she said, coming to my defense. "He's been really generous."

"So, what about your love life? Do you have a boyfriend?"

Karla answered, after a moment of hesitation, "I have a girlfriend."

Tony, for the first time, showed some interest in the conversation, expressed by turning briefly to look at Karla.

"A girlfriend?" Mio said.

"Yeah. Her name is Beanie. Beatrice, but she likes me to call her Beanie."

"Have you been together long?"

"About a year. I had a boyfriend before that, but, I don't know, turning tricks and all, it was hard."

"How so, exactly?"

"I couldn't keep it separated," Karla explained. "I'd have sex with guys for money, then I'd try to have sex with my boyfriend for pleasure, and, you know, for love. But I couldn't keep them apart in my head. All those shits who paid for it, I couldn't keep them out of my mind. Everything was sort of contaminated. You know what I mean?"

"And it's different with Beanie?" Mio asked.

"Yeah, it is. Being with Beanie, with a woman, lets me keep the two things completely separate. Sex for money was only with men, sex for love was, is, only with Beanie. They're completely different. They have nothing to do with one another."

"A sensible solution," Mio said, after briefly weighing the matter. "Since you don't seem to mind me prying into your private life, what does Beanie do?"

"When she isn't a complete mental wreck, she's an artist, a painter, and she's really talented, too."

"Has she sold many paintings?"

"That's where the mental wreck part comes in. She's never sold even one. But I know she will."

Mio looked at me, an unvoiced question in her expression. I answered with a barely noticeable shrug.

"Tony, do you have one of my gallery cards with you?"

Tony leaned sideways to get to his wallet. I thought the car

163

was going to change lanes. "For Karla?" he asked.

"Yes, thank you."

Tony handed Karla a business card, which she took and slipped into her jacket pocket.

"That's my gallery in Tokyo," Mio explained. "If you think Beanie would be interested, have her email some digital photos of her work."

"She'll be thrilled." Karla said.

"No promises," Mio cautioned. "I'll look at them. If I think they might sell in Japan, I'll have her ship a few pieces over, and we'll see what happens."

Mio was always the businesswoman, but I had a feeling there was something more going on.

•

It was a little after 10:00 when we exited the freeway into downtown San Francisco. We parked the car at a nearby garage and walked to Satellite. Not surprisingly, the doorman carded Mio, who looks about fourteen. He studied her driver's license long enough to let us know he wasn't fooled by it, then let us in. The club's interior consisted of a large, rectangular dance floor at street level, with raised balconies on the two sides, each with its own bar. The balconies were about three feet above the dance floor, with steps at the front on both sides, and tables lining their length. Padded railings ran along the balcony edges, providing patrons with a place to stand and watch the action, and preventing them from falling over the side as the evening progressed and they made whatever adjustments they considered appropriate to their blood chemistry. At the back, more steps led to a slightly higher balcony along the rear wall where a DJ manned an elaborate electronic sound studio. On each side of the DJ, larger tables were set in the corners. The club wasn't particularly crowded so we sat at one of the larger tables, giving us a fairly unobstructed view of the interior.

The music seemed to be convincing everyone they were having a good time, the volume high enough to prevent the brain from forming any thoughts to the contrary. A waitress came to the table and took our orders: club sodas for Mio and me, a beer for Tony, and Karla ordered something called a Screaming Orgasm.

"I know," she explained, yelling to be heard over the music, "it's a stupid name, but I love the taste. Irish Cream, Triple Sec, and Cognac."

Mio wasn't going to waste any time. "I'll be on the dance floor," she said, leaning toward Karla, "come and find me when you've had your Orgasm."

There was a doorway in the corner behind us leading to stairs down to the main level. Mio disappeared through the doorway, and a few seconds later I could see her dancing her way toward the center of the floor. Tony followed her progress, too. His behavior toward Mio was unmistakably fatherly, which was amusing considering she was about two hundred years older than he was.

Karla got up and stood at the rail, watching the dancers below. When the drinks arrived, she took hers back to the rail and drank it while standing. When she was finished, she sat the glass on the table, gave Tony and me a little wave, and headed after Mio.

Tony didn't usually say much, which was something I liked about him. Anyway, the noise level was too high for conversation. His attention was on the dance floor, and it looked like he was content to keep it there. Since entering the club, I'd had my eye out for large Ukrainian types, but so far hadn't seen anyone who fit that description. The crowd was made up for the most part of young professionals, people in their twenties and thirties. They looked like they had money, like they had devoted themselves to acquiring it, and having accomplished that, were now bereft of imagination. I suppose I wasn't being very charitable.

I hadn't expected to just walk into the club and bump into one of the Ukrainians, so what happened next was something of a surprise. Leave it to Mio to be the catalyst of the unexpected. I noticed that both she and Karla were attracting a certain amount of admiring attention from the other dancers. A small but noticeably disproportionate space had grown around the two of them as a result of the others watching. At one point, a young man, maybe in his late twenties, moved in between the two women, with the obvious intention of appropriating Karla. Mio simply danced around him, and as she did, Karla turned away from the guy, reestablishing her position with Mio. When the guy tried it a second time, Karla made an unequivocal gesture of dismissal and I could read her lips as she told him to fuck off. The guy stopped dancing and intentionally brushed her with his shoulder as he walked past. Karla lost her balance and almost fell.

Tony may have seen what happened next. I don't think anyone else did. While Karla was staggering to catch her balance, ninety-one pounds of haute couture blur flashed low and fast across the intervening space. Mio swung her right arm, driving the entire force of her body through her fist and into the side of the guy's right knee. There was a loud crack, probably not audible to human ears over the noise of the music, then a much louder scream that definitely was audible, and the guy went down. The best part came after Mio hit him. She spun around a full turn and a quarter in a kind of figure skating-kung fu-tango move, and melted inconspicuously back into the dancers. Neither the guy, nor anyone else around them, seemed to have a clue as to what had just happened. By the time Karla had regained her balance, Mio had calmly taken her by the arm and was walking her toward the stairs.

"Mother of God!" Karla said, when she got back to our table. "I need another drink!" She wiped the sweat off her forehead with a napkin and beckoned at a nearby waitress. "How about you, Tony? You want another beer?"

Tony nodded and Karla ordered his beer, along with another Screaming Orgasm for herself. She daubed more sweat off her face and looked at Mio. "Damn, woman! You haven't even broken a sweat!"

"Sweetheart," Mio said calmly, "I've barely warmed up."

Mio's words were directed to Karla, but her eyes were on me. I'd noticed the endearment, "sweetheart," but I was more interested in what was happening on the dance floor.

"What do you see, Shake?" Mio asked.

I had to admit, it was a little too good to be true. I stood up and moved to the rail for a better view. Mio followed. "The guy whose leg you tapped," I said, "you see the big guy helping him off the dance floor? When he turns, check out the back of his right hand."

The big guy was helping the injured man to the front of the club where a waitress had brought down a chair for him to sit on.

"Four-o-four," Mio said. "One of your Ukrainians?"

"Very possibly," I said, pointing. "He came through that door behind the bar."

The big guy was on his cell phone, probably calling an ambulance. The one with the knee problem was clearly in a lot of pain. He was gripping his injured leg by the thigh, his face constricted in agony, his head rocking forward and back as if he were emphatically answering a question no one was asking. The waitress who'd brought the chair had gone and come back with a glass of something strong for him to drink. Meanwhile, the guy with the tattoo had been joined by a second large specimen, also possibly Ukrainian, but younger and without the tattoo. These two milled around the front of the club until an ambulance pulled up outside. An EMT came in, assessed the situation, then radioed for her partner to bring in a wheel chair. When they'd rolled the guy out, the two maybe-Ukrainians went back through the door behind the bar.

"What do you want to do?" Mio asked.

It was a little after 11:30. The club closed at 2:00. "I think I'll just watch for a while, see if one of them leaves. If he does, depending on what time it is, Tony and Karla can stay here while we have a talk with him outside."

"And if they're both still here at 2:00?"

"Don't know yet. I'll think about it."

Mio and I returned to our table. I sat down but she wanted to dance some more.

"Rested up?" Mio asked Karla.

Karla had finished her drink and was eating the ice. "Maybe Tony would like to dance some?"

All three of us looked at Tony. His eyes moved slowly from Mio to Karla and back again. "I'm happy right here," he said.

"Tony's not too keen on dancing," Mio said. "His idea of a good time usually has something to do with fuel injection." She stood up and placed her hand on Karla's shoulder. "Come on. I want you to show me some of your moves."

18

Just before midnight, the tattooed Ukrainian came out from behind the bar. This time he was wearing a leather jacket. After a brief conversation with one of the bartenders, he started walking toward the front door.

"Tony," I said, leaning closer so he could hear, "Mio and I have to go out for a bit. It shouldn't take long. We'll either come back to the club when we're finished, or I'll call Karla's cell and you can come pick us up."

Tony nodded assent and I headed downstairs. The club was now packed, the music thunderous. About half way along the right balcony, I caught a clear view of Mio. In my normal speaking voice, I said her name. Thirty feet away, her eyes turned instantly to mine. I motioned with my head toward the front. She stopped dancing and beckoned Karla to come closer. Karla leaned down and she and Mio conferred briefly, then Mio turned and moved cat-like through the crowd of dancers.

At the door, I gave Mio her handbag and we left the club. The night had grown dead calm. The Ukrainian was about twenty yards away from us, headed, I guessed, to his car. There was no need to be surreptitious, so we followed, Mio taking my arm as if we were just another couple enjoying the local version of the good life. The guy's destination turned out to be the same garage where we were parked. He stopped in front of the street-level elevator, pressed the button and waited. Mio and I continued past him and into the stairwell. We paused at the bottom of the stairs, listening for the elevator to start its ascent, then went up following the sound. It stopped at level 4. We heard the doors open, then watched through a small window in the stairwell door as our Ukrainian emerged. I opened the door and followed Mio into the parking area.

Not far from the elevator, the Ukrainian aimed his electronic key at the long row of parked cars. A double beep followed by blinking taillights: a late model BMW about six cars further along marked our destination. Mio slipped silently away, moving fast and low along the front of the parked cars. I was only a few paces back, walking down the center of the driveway.

"Pardon me," I said, when the Ukrainian reached his car.

He stopped and turned around, but didn't say anything. He was a big one, six-two or three, probably two-sixty, or so, and lots of muscle. I thought I'd try being polite.

"Sorry to bother you, but I'm wondering if you might be able to help me with something." I stepped forward while saying this. There was something surprisingly mild-mannered about the guy. His size probably made him scary to most humans, but he didn't strike me as being volatile. I stepped closer and extended my hand. "My name is Shake."

He shook my hand, flinching slightly, probably at the temperature of my skin. "I am Levko."

"It's a pleasure, Levko."

I let go of his hand and took a step back, giving him some space to cooperate in. He glanced behind him and saw Mio standing next to his front bumper, her feet shoulder-width apart, hands hanging relaxed at her sides, so motionless she could have been cast in bronze. I noticed that she was not holding her purse, which meant, in all likelihood that she was holding her new knife. Her presence seemed to confuse Levko. His head kept snapping back and forth between Mio and me, as if it were operating independently of his volition.

"You're probably wondering if a big guy like yourself needs to be concerned about a woman, especially one her size." My voice compelled his head to stay turned toward me. "That's the primitive part of your brain trying to take over. You know, fight or flight? You don't want to listen to it, Levko. You need your higher faculties right now."

At that point, it was obvious we weren't there for a friendly chat.

"Am I supposed to be afraid of you and little girl?" he asked. He said this with a certain bravado, but when he glanced back at Mio, he jumped like he'd been goosed. Mio was standing in exactly the same posture, but closer, next to the driver's door.

"Be smart," I said, "and this will be easy for all of us."

People are peculiar creatures. If you tell them what the smart move is, sometimes, not often, but sometimes, they'll make it, just to prove they really are smart.

"What is this about?" he asked warily. "You are not cops?"

"We are not cops."

"Then I don't have to talk to you," he said, as if that settled the matter.

"You don't have to, Levko. But it would be better if you did."

"I want to go home now," he said, almost as if by saying it, he would be able to follow his own lead. But his feet weren't cooperating. Instead of moving toward his car door, he stepped around the front of the adjacent car, putting some additional space between himself and Mio. There was something slightly humorous and a little bit endearing in the discrepancy between

172

his words and his actions.

"You're not going to run home, are you?" I asked.

With Mio no longer directly behind him, he seemed a fraction more relaxed "What do you want?"

"Just some information." I said.

He was still looking at Mio, standing motionless as stone. "Is she alive?" he asked.

"More alive than you'll be if you play this wrong."

Direct threats like that generally increase the human male's flow of testosterone. I expected him to puff up, show us he wasn't afraid, and dare us to fuck with him. But that's not what happened. Instead, he looked me in the eye and I could see that he was frightened and tired and constitutionally disinclined to fight. "So ask your questions," he said.

"About a year ago, a Sacramento cop named Dean Arnaud was killed shortly after buying cocaine from a mutual acquaintance of ours."

"We did not kill cop," he exclaimed. "We are not criminals."

Something in the way he'd said it made me think he was telling the truth. "Who's 'we'?" I asked.

"Me and my cousin, Leo."

"Was he the one at the club who helped you with the injured guy?"

"Yes, that was Leo."

"When you say you didn't kill Arnaud, does that mean you didn't buy the coke from him?"

"We never bought anything from the cop."

"But you went to Sacramento to buy coke."

"Sometimes. To buy drugs from Danny Weiss. Not from

cop."

"Then who did Yavorsky send to meet Arnaud?"

Yavorsky's name seemed to surprise him. Or scare him. "If you know Yavorsky, you know I cannot tell you that." It was a cool evening, but he was starting to sweat. He wiped his forehead with the palm of his hand. "I cannot discuss this." The guy was genuinely distraught. He started to run his hands through his hair, but stopped midway, his hands clasping his head like he was trying to prevent it from opening.

"Are you afraid of Yavorsky?" I asked.

Levko laughed, but not because he thought it was funny. "If you are not afraid of him, it is because you don't know him. He has many powerful friends, here and in Ukraine. Bad men, like him. We, me and Leo, we have family in Ukraine. If we cross Yavorsky, he will hurt our family."

The odd thing was, I could see he wanted to talk, to get it all out. He just wasn't sure it was me he wanted to tell. The circumstances of his life had trapped him in a situation not at all to his liking, but he didn't know if I was a way out of the trap, or if I would only get him more deeply ensnared.

"I know you're in a tough spot, Levko. You don't want to do anything that will put your family in danger. I understand that. But you're going to have to tell us more."

"We are not criminals," he said again. "Leo is good man. He is studying at University to be engineer. He works part time at Satellite, as bouncer. He is big, like me, but nice guy. He is not killer. Yavorsky has someone else do his killing."

"This someone else is who he sent to meet Arnaud?"

He looked at Mio again, who still had not moved. "She is making me very nervous."

When he said this, Mio folded her arms across her chest, turned and leaned her back against the door of his car, then proceeded to examine one her shoes.

"Who killed Arnaud, Levko?"

"His name is Nikolai Beketov. He is ex-Soviet Army. Very bad. Very dangerous."

"Does he live here in San Francisco?"

"No. He is gone. Back to Ukraine. He only comes to States when Yavorsky calls him."

"Why did Yavorsky want Arnaud killed? That's a lot of bother and expense to bring this guy all the way from Ukraine."

"I am not positive," he said, sighing like an exhausted bear.

"None of this will get back to Yavorsky, Levko. Just tell me what happened."

"A year or so ago, this guy, Arnaud, he came to Satellite with picture of young girl, asking people, employees and customers, did they know her. He showed me picture. He said girl was his niece and he was trying to find her."

"And you recognized her from somewhere?"

"Yes. Yavorsky sells young girls. Boys, too, sometimes. But mostly girls. They are taken to Mexico, then to Middle East somewhere, I think. Or maybe India. I am not sure. But sometimes they are delivered to guy here, in California. He lives in mountains, near Pollock Pines. The girl in picture, she was delivered to Pines Guy. That's what I call him, Pines Guy."

"How do you know? Did you and your cousin deliver her?"

"Not Leo. He knows nothing about this. I delivered girl."

He looked like he was going to start crying. "So after

175

Arnaud showed you the girl's photo, what happened?"

"I told Yavorsky. I think he told Pines Guy. After that, I am not sure. Maybe Pines Guy paid Yavorsky to kill cop. Or maybe Yavorsky did it on his own. But Beketov was here, in San Francisco."

It was all starting to make a certain twisted sense. "What about this Pines Guy?" I asked.

"I don't know anything about him. I don't even know his name. He is just Pines Guy. He must be rich, I think, to buy girls. And he has big house."

"How many girls have you delivered there?" I asked.

He didn't have to think to answer. His conscience had been keeping track. "Five."

"Over how long a period?"

"About two years."

"Have you ever seen any of them again, after you delivered them? Did you see any of the first girls when you delivered the later ones?"

"Never. I always make deliveries late at night. House is always dark. I only saw Pines Guy."

Arnaud probably didn't have any idea what happened to his niece. His snooping around just made these guys nervous enough to have him disposed of. It didn't sound good for the girl. Levko's head was jerking back and forth again between Mio and me.

"Levko, do you have regular days off?"

"I am off Monday and Tuesday," he answered, as affably as if he thought I might invite him bowling.

"Good. Here's what I'd like you to do. This coming Monday evening, the day after tomorrow, I want you to drive to

Sacramento and pick me up at 9:00 p.m. at the Hyatt Regency. It's across the street from the capitol. Do you know where that is?"

"Yes, I know."

"We'll take a little drive and you can show me where this Pines Guy lives."

Levko forced his hands into his pants pockets and started shaking his head. He looked like a sullen, recalcitrant teenager. "I am sorry, but I won't go near Pines Guy."

"I just want you to show me where his house is. That's all. After that, you can drive me back to Sacramento and I'll leave you alone."

I waited while he thought about it, but he was taking too long.

"I'm making it easy for you, Levko. This way, Yavorsky and Beketov are left out of it."

"I will show you," he said, after another bear sigh.

It was a little weird, his being so accommodating. I'd anticipated having to get nasty. Levko really was in the wrong line of work. "Why are you working for someone like Yavorsky?" I asked.

"In Ukraine I was farmer. My family is poor. I don't have skills here, in America. Yavorsky is evil fuck but he pays good money, so I can help family in Ukraine."

Mio moved silently back the way she'd come. "Good night, Levko," I said, turning to leave. "Monday, 9:00 p.m."

He hadn't noticed Mio leave and was briefly confused when he saw that she was no longer leaning on his car. He opened the door, but hesitated before getting in, scanning the garage, looking for her. When he saw her standing next to the elevator, their eyes locked for just a second before he scrambled into his car and drove away.

•

Karla had had a couple more drinks in our absence, so Tony drove us back to Sacramento. I sat up front, Karla and Mio rode in the back. We were hardly on the bridge crossing the bay before Karla was asleep. She had leaned over to lie down with her head on Mio's lap. When I looked back, Mio was absently stroking Karla's hair. She looked my way briefly, her face expressionless, then turned her eyes back to the night.

I knew Mio was neither sentimental nor the least bit maternal. One night, many years ago, I had watched while she drank the blood of two of the cutest little six-year-old twin girls. Her only comment after she was finished was that even their blood tasted identical. She often expressed affection for humans with whom she maintained various relations, but as far as I could tell, her behavior was part of a general strategy of resource management, rather than an expression of genuine affection. All of which made me wonder what was behind the camaraderie that seemed to have developed so quickly between her and Karla. I also knew that any discussion of the matter would be at Mio's instigation.

Karla woke up as we were arriving back in Sacramento. I told her I'd be needing her services again sometime toward the end of the coming week, and I would give her a call. She moved up front to drive when Mio and I got out at the footbridge. On the walk back to the house, Mio asked if I wanted her to accompany me to Pollock Pines. She had told me earlier she was planning to leave Sunday evening, so I said it wasn't necessary. As things turned out, it was probably just as well that she was leaving.

19

At nine o'clock on Monday evening, I was standing near the lobby entrance of the Hyatt when Levko drove up in his BMW. If providing financial assistance to his family back in Ukraine was a hardship, it wasn't preventing him from cultivating his image here in the States. He saw me and stopped at the curb, hardly looking at me when I got in.

From downtown Sacramento, Pollock Pines was less than an hour's drive up Highway 50. The night was clear and cold. California was having another dry year. It was the middle of December, and there was hardly any snow in the mountains. We drove for fifteen or twenty minutes before Levko spoke.

"Your woman friend?" he said.

I wasn't sure at first if it had been a statement or a question. "She left last night, to Mexico, on business. Were you hoping to see her again?"

He made a little choking sound. "After tonight, I will not see *you* again, right?"

He'd had some time to think since Saturday. I wondered how close he'd come to not showing up. "This isn't so bad, is it, just taking me for a drive?"

"You do not know Yavorsky. He is nut case. Really crazy when he is mad. If he knew I showed you Pines Guy's house, I think maybe... I don't know... it would not be good for me."

Levko seemed genuinely concerned, but I didn't think there was much danger of Yavorsky finding out what we were up to. Levko, I assumed, felt the same way, otherwise he would have put up more resistance. "Does he know you're here, in Sacramento?" I asked.

"No. It is my day off. He does not watch so close."

"Then there shouldn't be any problem."

There wasn't much traffic on I-50 at that time of night. The commuters had all long since returned to their little castles in the foothills. I hadn't been in the Sacramento area long enough to witness the spread of its suburban communities, but the process is similar everywhere. Once a city's more centrally located areas have reached a density that either leads to over-congestion and decay or prohibitive property values, or both, the new money moves to the periphery. The periphery expands outward with each migration, spawning larger and more expensive homes. Developers market these communities to appeal to egos delusional with new wealth. The communities offer a kind of landed-gentry fantasy that appeals to the young, upwardly mobile professionals eager to display their superiority through flamboyant possessions. They can sleep soundly in their gated communities, safe behind their high-tech security systems, confident that their neighbors, though they my be borderline psychotics, are not dangerous in virtue of disparities in wealth.

The night grew colder as we climbed out of the valley. Levko made another in a series of fine adjustments to the car's heater. Watching him drive, it was clear he was emotionally attached to his car. There was the obvious ego aspect of it, using the car to project his self-image; the sexy side of power, speed, luxury craftsmanship. But there was also the more tangible, tactile side of operating the car. The physical manipulation of its various parts brought the car's power under human control and gave the machine its symbiotic seductiveness. It was, I suppose, an ideal choice as a status symbol. But if cars didn't exit, something else would have served the same purpose. When your self-image is nine-tenths wishful thinking, you need a way to prop it up.

Mio once told me an interesting anecdote that occurred in Japan during the Tokugawa Shogunate. The official class structure of Japan was Confucian, which placed merchants at the bottom of the social scale. The merchants, however, did what merchants tend to do. They got rich. And they displayed their wealth the way the wealthy do: ostentatiously. Naturally enough, they used their clothing as a symbol of their elite status. They decorated themselves in sumptuous fabrics as an advertisement of their true social standing and a direct challenge to the Shogunate's professed Confucian values. They were supposed to be at the bottom, but their growing wealth had gradually inverted the Confucian totem pole.

So what did the government do? They outlawed flamboyant clothes. Whenever in public view, merchants were required to dress in very plain garments. What did the merchants do? They complied, of course. They had money, but the Shogun had swords. However, being the clever men they were, they complied only with the letter of the law. They turned their garments inside out, so the sumptuous fabrics became the inner linings. Whenever they needed to display their privileged status, they could simply open their garments and strut like peacocks.

Levko's voice brought me back from Japan. "Why are you interested in cop's murder?" he asked.

I could have fed him a line, making up something plausible. Or I could have told him it wasn't any of his concern.

But there was something genuinely affable about this big Ukrainian. I found myself taking a simpler tack. "I didn't know the guy or his niece. Never met them. My interest is through Arnaud's wife."

"We're you having affair?"

"Nothing that banal. My relationship with Francine Arnaud was brief and somewhat adventitious to all of this."

"Adventitious?"

"Coincidental."

"So why all the trouble?"

"Considering our agreement, Levko, it's probably better if we don't go into that."

"OK," he said, shrugging. "But seems like big hassle."

"Is this a big hassle for you?" I asked.

"Not so much. I like driving. But my girlfriend is suspicious. She is jealous type. She wants to know everywhere I go."

"I take it you made something up?"

"I told her I was going to pick up stuff I bought on eBay," he said, smiling, obviously pleased by the cleverness of his subterfuge.

"She didn't want to come?"

"No. I told her it was Teddy Roosevelt stuff."

"Teddy Roosevelt?"

"Yes. Teddy is my favorite president. I am collector. But girlfriend thinks it is stupid waste of money."

There were probably stranger hobbies for a Ukrainian immigrant, but nothing came immediately to mind. "Roosevelt isn't your girlfriend's favorite president?" I asked.

He looked at me like it was a perfectly reasonable

question. "Girlfriend is American," he said, as if that were a sufficient explanation.

"I see," I said. "She's not interested in history."

"She is smart woman. But Ukrainian farmer has better education."

We took the Sly Park exit off 50, crossed the highway and went north, winding along Canyon Edge Road, then turned on Boyce Canyon Road. A mile or so further, approaching a sharp bend, Levko pulled off the pavement and stopped.

"You can see Pines Guy's house from here."

He opened his door and got out. I followed him across the road to a vantage point. From where we stood, the land fell off abruptly about two hundred feet down to the bottom of a ravine. I could hear water gurgling in a small creek at the bottom. Beyond the creek, the bank rose steeply for thirty feet or so, then angled to a gentler slope as it climbed the far side of the ravine.

"He lives there," Levko said, pointing to some lights about a quarter mile away, visible through the trees.

There was enough moonlight to make out the shadowed contours of a large, two story house. It looked like there were also two detached structures. One was probably a garage. The other, some kind of shed, was larger and farther away from the house.

"The lights are all outside," I said. "The house looks dark."

"House is always dark when I come. But I think Pines Guy is home. You can't see house from where driveway meets road. You have to go up driveway. I don't want to do that. I don't want Pines Guy to see me and tell Yavorsky."

I had no problem with that. There was no reason for me to get Levko in trouble with his boss. "When you brought the girls here," I asked, "did you see anyone else around the house?"

"Never. Only Pines Guy."

"Did you go inside?"

"No. Pines Guy came out to my car and took girls. One time I asked him if I could use bathroom. He said bears shit in woods."

It would have been nice to get a closer look at the house, but I'd made a deal with Levko. "Let's drive a little further. I want to see where his driveway meets the road."

We walked back to the car. About a half mile further, Levko pointed out an unmarked, narrow, dirt drive, partially overgrown with weeds. It would be easy to miss if you didn't know where it was.

The drive back to Sacramento was uneventful. I learned a little more than I really wanted to know about Teddy Roosevelt. I also learned something interesting about Richardson. According to Levko, Yavorsky and Richardson had known each other for a long time. Not friends, exactly, but their business connections went back several years. Richardson was going to be disappointed to hear that his December payment would be doubled.

20

The following Wednesday evening I went to the university library. I've always liked libraries. In the age of the Internet, their solid inefficiency has a distinctive charm. I like to stroll casually through the library stacks, slide an interesting title off the shelf and thumb leisurely through its pages. That's what I was doing Wednesday evening. I wasn't looking for anything in particular, just pausing at whatever caught my eye. I found a fascinating photo collection of wildly extravagant marine life. The quality of the photographs was exceptional. Looking at these bizarre creatures, I was amazed at what evolution could do with living tissue. I also found an interesting work on the early Mamluk slave soldiers of Baghdad. They were almost as bizarre as the sea creatures.

I left the library a few minutes before eleven. The evening was cool and overcast, the ground wet from a light sprinkle. The clouds seemed to be moving much faster than the light breeze circulating between campus buildings. It was one of those nights when the weather was peaceful on the ground, but turbulent at higher altitude. The breeze picked up a little as I moved out of the protection of the buildings, but not much. I followed the bike path to the footbridge crossing the American River and started across. A solitary man was standing at the rail near the center of the bridge, staring into the darkness below. He was wearing a long wool overcoat that looked expensive, but old and a little tattered. Faded sweat pants emerged from below the coat, billowing shapelessly around the elastic at his ankles. A tattered pair of Top-Siders served for shoes, and on his head he was wearing a Lahinch, one of those small-brimmed, fabric hats popular among bird-watcher types and Asian tourists.

As I approached, he looked my way, a bit longer than a glance, long enough to do the sort of quick assessment a man might make when being approached by a stranger at night. Whatever the assessment told him, it didn't seem to cause concern. He turned back to the river and his private thoughts. I expected him to ignore me as I passed and was surprised when he spoke.

"Time is a river which carries me along, but I am the river."

I stopped. "Borges, if I'm not mistaken."

"A Borges fan," he said, turning toward me, smiling.

"I am, though I like his fiction more than his poetry."

"Yes," he said, thoughtfully, "I suppose most people do." He scrutinized me for a moment. "If you don't mind my saying so, you don't look like a lit professor."

"I'll take that as a compliment."

"Indeed," he said, then raised and spread his arms, clearly amused by the state of his attire. "I, on the other hand, might very well pass for an aging academic. I'm obviously too muddleheaded to dress myself properly."

I've always found something admirable in the ability to laugh at oneself. "As far as I know," I said, "this bridge doesn't have a dress code."

He produced a short, laugh-like spurt that sounded like he'd hiccuped in the middle of a cough.

"Are you an aging academic?" I asked.

"Exactly half right," he announced cheerfully. "I'm aging,

even as we speak."

I stepped up to the guardrail beside him. "I trust the aging process is running at the normal speed? I'm not going to have to watch you decompose, am I?"

He laughed heartily. "One can only hope. But I'll tell you what, if I should stop talking and start to smell suspicious, you have my permission to drop me off the bridge."

It was my turn to laugh.

He offered me his hand. "My name's Steven."

"Shake," I said, taking his hand, my name causing the usual confusion. "My name is Shake," I clarified.

"That's a very cold paw you have there, Shake. Are you all right?"

"Quite all right, thanks," I said, remembering I would be needing some fresh blood before too long. "It's just poor circulation. It runs in the family."

We stood silently for a minute or two, both leaning against the guardrail, gazing into the darkness below the bridge.

"It's different at night," he said, breaking the silence. "In the daylight the river looks so inviting, but at night it's the opposite, forbidding."

"You find it inviting in daylight?"

"I do. I've always been attracted to bodies of water. Not the ocean, so much. It's too big and too spooky. But creeks, rivers, lakes, if they're clean, of course. I always have a powerful urge to dive in."

"I prefer a drier environment," I said.

"Well, it's not like I'm good for much in the water. I can swim, if we're generous in defining what that means. There's nothing very elegant about it. It's more like a desperately awkward refusal to drown."

I could imagine what that awkward thrashing might look like, and the image struck me as one generally applicable to humans, in or out of water; an awkward refusal to succumb to the inevitable.

"Do you often walk at night?" he asked.

"I find the night more congenial. I seem to be nocturnal by nature."

"I suppose the night must have its charms for me, too. I certainly spend a lot of time wandering around in the dark."

"Literally or figuratively?" I asked.

"A bit of both," he said, somewhat pensively.

A young man and woman were crossing the bridge on bicycles. Students, judging from their conversation. They were arguing about whether or not to buy an essay off the Internet. Steven and I stood quietly as they passed.

"Are you religious?" he asked, then sensing my aversion to the question, added, "Me neither," and brushed the air with his hand, as if swatting at an insect.

"People who aren't religious," I said, "don't generally spring that question on complete strangers."

"No, I suppose not." he agreed. "I'm not sure why I asked you that. I was just thinking about my mother when you happened by. She was a real Bible-pounder. A Southern Baptist. Ignorant and a bit violent, and since she couldn't actually quote the Bible, her Bible-pounding tended to take the form of pounding with the Bible. I can remember more than once being clobbered upside the head with her large-print King James."

I laughed again. "Like in the movies, when the suspect is getting the good cop/bad cop treatment, and the bad cop comes up behind him and clocks him with a phone book."

"Exactly. Same methodology, except she was both cops."

"So contact with the Bible dislodged your faith?"

"An appropriately comical way to describe it."

"And now? What? Are you having second thoughts?"

"No, no. Nothing like that," he assured me. "The idea of God gets more implausible the older I get."

"Like the tooth fairy," I suggested, wondering where this was leading. "If I were you, I wouldn't expect to be patted on the back for my powers of discrimination."

Steven slapped the metal guardrail with the palm of his hand. The ringing reverberated along the length of the bridge. "You're a quick study, Shake," he said, chuckling to himself. "But our accomplishments should be measured by the ruler of our abilities, don't you think?"

"Fair enough," I granted.

"And anyway," he said, "don't you think there's a difference between believing in the tooth fairy and believing in God?"

"It does seem to be easier for people to let go of the tooth fairy."

Steven rubbed his chin, the way he might have stroked his goatee if he'd had one. "It's hard, isn't it, to talk about religion?"

"People generally just want you to agree with them," I said.

"Yes, I suppose they do. In a way, maybe that's what the whole smoke and mirror show is about. Getting people to agree."

"Maybe," I said. "But there's an awful lot of disagreement between all these people trying to agree."

"Maybe that's the game. You win by getting the other guy to agree with you. After all, that's what everyone wants more of, isn't it?"

"Power, you mean?"

"Or as I prefer to call it, authority. We all want authority. We don't necessarily want to be global dictators, but we do want to have authority over whatever circumscribed domain happens to be under our sway. That domain may have grand dimensions, or be as small as the desk we sit behind five days a week in some dreary office. We may have the authority to influence millions, or we may be reduced to hounding our spouse into some exhausted state of acquiescence. We may have authority over entire nations, or our sovereignty may be limited to the arrangement of knickknacks on the mantel."

"Yes," I said, "and people are usually willing to throttle one another over the placement of their knickknacks."

"Just like my mother," he said.

"Why do think that was so important to her?"

"She was afraid, I suppose. I don't think the religion itself meant that much to her. She didn't try to understand it, or make sense of it. The world was a scary place for her, and she needed to believe something would protect her. Or at least give her some solace. That's why she needed the people around her to agree with her, so she could feel like her beliefs gave her some degree of control. And that's why she got violent when I didn't agree."

"So pounding you with the Bible was how she arranged the knickknacks on her mantel? That was her way of expressing her authority?"

"That's basically it, I think. She wasn't very bright.

Religion was the only way for her to have authority over anyone else. God is just so convenient."

"Convenient?" I asked.

"For many people, I think, God is the easiest way to acquire authority. Think about it. God allows you to possess the truth, and your authority can't be challenged by anyone, no matter how smart, powerful, educated, successful or rich they may be. Your authority is backed by a supreme being, so you can pretty much believe whatever you want. As a friend of mine once put it, an authority doesn't have to be an authority to be an authority."

"Come again?"

"Someone in a position of authority doesn't have to be a true authority. They don't actually have to know what they're talking about, in order to play the role of an authority, and to enjoy the privileges and influence that role gives them. Priests are a perfect example. They just have to play the part convincingly. The dimmest fundamentalists can defy the greatest scientific minds in the world. Why? Because God is the ultimate tool for establishing false authority."

"So what you're saying is that religious belief is really just a way for people to impose their will on one another?"

"Well," he said, waving his hand back and forth in a give-or-take gesture, "you know, it's never as simple as you'd like it to be. But, basically, yes. I don't think people really need to believe in God as much as they need to be right. They need to believe in themselves. So they become authorities on God. Then they can arrange their knickknacks just the way they want them, and to hell with anyone who says they're out of order."

"It sounds like you've got your knickknacks in order," I

said.

Steven lapsed into a thoughtful silence, then broke the silence with a chuckle. "I talk a lot sometimes," he said, sighing, "but in the end it doesn't add up to much."

"What would you like it to add up to?" I asked.

"Yes," he said, without hesitation.

I wasn't sure if he'd understood my question. "I beg your pardon?"

"Yes," he repeated. "I'd like it to add up to 'yes.'"

"I don't mean to be obtuse," I said, unable to follow his train of thought.

"All my life," he said, "I've been saying 'no' to things; to very nearly everything. But at the same time, always searching for something to say 'yes' to."

"I gather you haven't found it?"

"Well, I'm not sure, really. I tend to make the mistake of thinking I know what I'm looking for. And in a way, I do. But in a way, I don't. Not really."

"So the things you find don't meet your expectations?" I asked.

"Usually not. But that doesn't necessarily mean I'm disappointed. Sometimes the things we find are much more important than the things we're looking for."

"True enough," I said, knowing from experience that the things we find are sometimes unthinkable beforehand. "What might it be like, this thing you want to say 'yes' to?"

"Well, now, how can I put this? Let's say there is something I would like to experience before I die. It's not easy to describe, but maybe you'll know what I mean. I'm sixty-two years old, and one thing I've noticed about my life is that I've nearly always been wrong about the things that really matter. At any point in my life, looking back at an earlier time, I'd see that I was pretty consistently wrong. I'd make corrections in my thinking. But when I'd look back from some later time, I'd see that those corrections were also wrong. At sixty-two, I look back and see a life of misdeeds based on dubious judgments and half-baked ideas. I'm a bit like a wind-up toy that keeps falling over, pointlessly jerking its limbs while its spring runs down."

"In other words, you're a human being," I suggested.

"Perhaps you're right," he said, grinning. "The truth is, in spite of everything, I'm hopelessly optimistic."

Steven danced a little three-hundred-sixty-degree jig to demonstrate.

"So you think it may not be too late? You think you still might find what you've been looking for?"

"Since you seem to be willing to listen, I'll tell you a little story. When I was around twenty years old, I was a very conventional kid. Along with most other things, I had conventional, white-middle-class taste in music. I liked popular rock bands like The Doors, Hendrix, Cream, that sort of thing. One day I paid a visit to the home of a guy I'd recently met at college. He had studied music, played classical guitar, and his tastes were somewhat more sophisticated than mine. At his suggestion, we listened to an album he'd just recently acquired and was obviously excited about: Miles Davis At Fillmore. Are you familiar at all with Miles?"

"That was a landmark album," I said.

"You know it. Good. Anyway, I sat for the duration of the album, wondering what the hell this grinding cacophony of noise had to do with music. It was obvious to my friend that I didn't get it. I must have looked like I'd bitten into a turd, or something. I was glad when the album ended, but a little embarrassed, too.

"Later that day, I started thinking about the experience, wondering why I'd only heard noise when my friend had obviously heard music. I was sure nobody in their right mind would willingly subject themselves to that kind of auditory punishment. But it was also obvious that a concert hall full of people had paid to do just that. There had to be something I was missing. By evening, I was so obsessed I went to Tower Records and bought the LP. I took it home, put it on the stereo and listened again. And again. After a second and third hearing, it was still just an irritating, jumbled racket. There were stretches of rhythmic consistency, bits of melody here and there, but it just didn't come together. Still, I was determined. Then on the fourth try, about half way through the album, something clicked and I could hear it. Not only hear it, I was dumbstruck by how amazing, how beautiful it was."

I suspected Steven was attributing more importance to the experience than it really merited. "That kind of thing isn't so unusual, is it? You've probably had other similar experiences in your life, especially when you were a kid. Maybe everyone does. It reminds me of those optical illusions, like the duck/rabbit. Depending on how you look at it, your brain will interpret the image either as a duck looking in one direction or as a rabbit looking in the opposite direction."

"You're right, I think. But the point isn't so much that the brain can process the same data in very different ways. In my jazz experience, one way of hearing the sounds was chaotic and ugly and the other way was ordered and beautiful. At first there was an absence of something. Then that absence was filled with beauty. With the duck/rabbit, either way, all I have is a rough sketch of a duck or a rabbit. Neither enriches my life. Neither offers any deep aesthetic pleasure. With the music, it was the beginning of an enduring love of jazz. But more importantly, what changed was something inside myself. I was suddenly able to do something that a moment before I could not do. Something happened up here," he said, tapping the side of his head.

"And that," I asked, not intending to sound skeptical, "makes you optimistic that something similar will happen again? Like what? Enlightenment?"

"Well," he said, chuckling, "perhaps not enlightenment. That might be setting my sights a little too high. Maybe just a more comprehensive, more harmonious way of ordering my experience. The world is a lot like Miles was before I could hear it. Most of it seems ugly and chaotic. But that could just be me. Maybe it's really ordered and beautiful in a way I just can't see, yet."

"How old did you say you were?"

"Yes, I know," he sighed. "It's getting rather late in the game. But it doesn't seem so outlandish. I suppose all it really comes down to is being right about the world in some better, more useful way, so that when the unexpected happens, my opinions and beliefs, whatever knowledge and wisdom I have, are not undermined. I want the world to surprise me, but without pulling the rug out from under me."

"It's not easy having it both ways."

"But with luck I think you can. That's where my optimism kicks in. Despite all indications to the contrary, I have to tell myself there is a positive side to being sixty-two. I've had sixty-two years to listen to the world's noise. Something could still click up here," he said, tapping the side of his head again, "and I could start hearing music. Experience a kind of phase transition. Be able to see a little deeper into the world's depths."

"I don't mean to disabuse you," I said, "but it's been my experience that when people think they're plumbing the depths, what they're really doing is losing touch with the surface. As the poet, Homero Aridjis, once wrote, 'What we weave in solitude is unraveled by the doorbell's ringing.'"

"I like that," he said, chuckling. "I realize I probably sound a little deranged. As if all I have to do is fill my head with more and more noise, and sooner or later, magically or what have you, some higher level of organization will emerge. It sounds a little crazy to me, too. But maybe it isn't. Maybe everything will come together in a new way."

"The sum will become greater than the parts."

"Exactly. The sum will become greater than the parts."

"So, how is it looking, so far?"

"So far?" he repeated, with a wry smile. "So far the sum still seems to be a little less than the parts."

•

I continued my walk home, leaving Steven to his inner orchestrations. Our conversation had been oddly soothing, in a way I didn't often experience with humans. The feeling surprised me a little, if for no other reason than the fact that Steven seemed to be putting his faith in a pipe dream. He wasn't ignorant or stupid, but what he'd come up with left him hanging by a very slender thread. So slender, in fact, that blind faith and perverse optimism were the only things keeping it from snapping. At sixty-two, he was holding out for an epiphany that, if it came, would have to emerge out of the sheer complexity of his mental life. How was that for an act of faith?

On the other hand, I had to give him credit. The only way most people seem to be able to console themselves is by sabotaging their own critical faculties. They have to dull themselves down to avoid being eviscerated by their own gullibility. There may have been something inherently paradoxical about Steven's idea that he could stuff himself with knowledge and thereby arrive at enlightenment. As if by piling up enough debris, he could clear the way to his goal. But maybe it wasn't impossible. The world was full of surprises. I was a good example of a seemingly miraculous transformation.

In the end, Steven and I weren't all that different. We both wanted the clarity of a better story. His optimism may have been perverse, but perhaps no more so than my determination to find convincing reasons for who and who not to kill. Maybe we were both clutching at straws. Maybe we were both just giving ourselves something to do while our clocks ran down. The difference was that his clock was going to stop a lot sooner than mine. It would have been nice if becoming a vampire increased my clarity as much as it increased my strength and speed, but it didn't. It just gave me a lot more time to stumble around in.

·

I was nearing my house when I saw two cats squared off against each other, one on each side of a row of small junipers demarcating the boundary between adjacent front lawns. I slowed my pace as I drew nearer, hearing the tension boiling to a hiss in these two ferocious, supposedly domesticated animals. One of the cats suddenly leapt forward, his adversary meeting him in a screeching ball of fur, claws and teeth. This lasted about half a second before the loser took off at full speed, the victor close on his tail.

The cats had been too preoccupied to notice my presence, and both came across the lawn straight at me. Bits of grass flew into the air as the first cat saw me and clawed its way through a high-speed ninety-degree turn. It was a nice move. The second cat had a bit more time to negotiate and veered in pursuit. I stepped forward and snatched up the little demon by the scruff of its neck. Holding it away from my body, I watched as it tried to free itself, slashing the air with its extended claws. I thought about my conversation with Steven, wondering if complexity might really offer solutions that simplicity lacked. Wasn't it better to keep things simple? Could you ever get the soup right just by tossing more and more stuff into the pot?

I gave the cat a gentle toss. It landed as cats will, and darted into the night.

21

The weather cleared over the weekend. I'd given Karla a call on Sunday and arranged to be picked up the following evening at 11:00 p.m. I suggested that she dress warmly because she might have to wait for me in the car and I wasn't sure how long I would be. Monday night was clear, cold and windy. It would be colder still at the higher altitude of Pollock Pines. I wore a long sleeved black jersey made of some kind of microfiber under a dark blue nylon windbreaker.

Karla was right on time. She'd dressed warmly, as I'd suggested, wearing a heavy wool sweater under her leather jacket, what looked like logging boots, and some kind of fur-lined, leather head piece reminiscent of an old-fashioned aviator's helmet, complete with dangling ear flaps.

"I know," she said, "I look like a beagle. But it keeps my ears warm." She examined my attire while she was saying this, her expression mildly incredulous. "Is that your idea of dressing for the weather?"

"According to the ads, this shirt is a wonder fabric. Very popular among the mountain-climbing set, as well as with car-campers who want the technical look. Under the windbreaker it's surprisingly warm."

Karla looked momentarily dubious, but dropped the subject to focus on her driving. We took Howe Avenue to I-50 and headed east toward the Sierras. Karla seemed quieter than normal, but after a few minutes she broke the silence.

"How's Mio doing?" she asked.

"She's fine, I'm sure."

"She said she was going to Mexico."

I was still curious about the intimacy they'd so quickly acquired.

"She told me at the club in San Francisco," Karla explained, as if sensing my curiosity.

"She seems to have taken a liking to you."

"You think?" she asked, after a long thoughtful pause.

"I've known Mio for a long time. Trust me, she likes you."

"I like her, too. But, I don't know, she seems so..."

"What?" I asked.

"I don't know. I guess she makes me feel something I'm not used to feeling around other people."

"Oh? What's that?"

She changed her grip on the steering wheel, as if she needed to brace herself for the admission. "Inadequate."

"Mio has a very forceful personality," I said. "She takes some getting used to."

"You know," she said, "I'm not blind or stupid." She gave me one of those looks designed to make it clear that she wasn't fooled by my evasions. "I didn't see what happened, but I know it was Mio who broke that guy's leg at Satellite."

"You're probably right," I said, still reluctant to get tangled up in an explanation. "But I suspect he had it coming."

My attempt to deflect further questions was only half-hearted. On the one hand, I didn't want to start an explanation I wouldn't be able to finish. But on the other hand, I was curious about how Karla rationalized the things she witnessed around Mio and me. She obviously wanted to keep her job, and that meant turning a blind eye to things that might otherwise frighten her away. But eventually she would cross a threshold beyond which the power of denial would no longer shield her. What would happen then was anyone's guess.

"I don't often give advice," I said. "But since this has to do with Mio, I'll offer a word of caution. If you should ever tell her that you're going to do something, make sure you do it. Everything else will take care of itself."

"That sounds a little ominous."

"I don't mean it to. It's just that, as things stand, you can count Mio as your friend, and that makes you very lucky. Believe me, it's far preferable to having her as an enemy."

Karla looked deeply puzzled. "Is that supposed to ease my mind?" she asked.

"Ease of mind wasn't exactly what I was aiming at."

The tension broke and she chuckled. "If you don't mind my saying so, Shake, you're very calculating."

"I suppose I am at times," I admitted. "People tend to blunder through things, as if they were trying to make their lives interesting through mishaps. Mostly avoidable mishaps. You're really not like that, even if it seems to you at times that you are."

"Yeah," she agreed, "like most of the time."

"It only seems that way, Karla. You're a smart girl. You have a wild streak, but the fact is, you're cautious even when you're wild. And that's good. Especially where Mio is concerned. She's not something you want to blunder into."

Karla's eyes were fixed on the road, but her mind was no doubt swarming with questions I wasn't eager to be asked.

"It's good to maintain a degree of detachment," I continued, "because you can never be sure what's at stake. You never really know what's riding on your actions. None of us ever knows."

"You're sounding ominous again," she said, though without the tension in her voice.

We were just passing through the Folsom area, where the freeway still paralleled the American River. In the mid-nineteenth century, right around the time of my human birth, the land along the river had all of its soil washed away through hydraulic mining. The miners took the gold and left mounds of boulders neatly spaced for miles, like a storage yard of smooth, head-sized rocks. A hundred and fifty years later, many of these mounds were still visible, covered with whatever grass and shrubs were able to fix their roots in the thin soil that had collected between the stones.

"Could I could ask you a question, Shake?"

"You can ask."

"What do you do? For a job, I mean. For money?"

"I don't do anything for money," I said. "Not in the conventional sense, anyway. I don't have to."

"So you're just, like, rich?"

"By some standards. I have enough money not to have to worry about it."

Karla seemed distracted, as if she wasn't really listening to what I'd said.

"I have the feeling there's something else on your mind," I ventured.

"Shit!" she said, shaking her head. "On top of everything else, I hope you're not psychic, too."

"Ask whatever you want, Karla."

"I don't want you to take this the wrong way," she began. "I'm not having second thoughts about the job, or anything like that."

"Okay."

"I just have this feeling, like, at some level I'm not used to feeling, that you're... I don't know, dangerous."

"You don't have to worry about that, Karla. Like I told you, I'm on your side."

"I believe you, Shake. I'm not sure why, but I do. And maybe that's what gives me the courage to keep this job. But, to be honest, that's not the question I really wanted to ask."

I didn't say anything, just gave her the time she needed to get to what was bothering her.

"This may sound weird, but is Mio as dangerous as you are?"

I could see then that Mio had made a very deep impression on Karla. Not that I was surprised. Mio was like a knife. A knife so sharp that it could only cut deeply. "I told you when you took the job that I wouldn't bullshit you. I may refuse to answer a question, but if I do answer, I'll tell you the truth, in so far as I can."

"You can tell me the truth. I can handle it."

Maybe so, I thought. But then, people so often think they can handle reality, right up to the moment it buries them like an avalanche. I must have been taking too long to consider my answer.

"So," Karla asked, interrupting my thoughts, "is she as dangerous as you are?"

"In all honesty, I would have to say Mio is considerably more dangerous."

Karla was quiet for a long time. When she spoke, it was as if she'd resolved something for herself. "Thank you, Shake," she said. "I just needed to ask."

•

We took the Sly Park exit off I-50. There were motels and an all-night convenience store near the exit.

"I don't want a repeat of our Sloughhouse adventure," I said, "so I suggest you come back here after you drop me off. I didn't see a 24-hour restaurant nearby, but you can park for a while by that convenience store."

"I could use some coffee, anyway," Karla said. "How long is this going to take?"

"I don't know. Probably not long. If you feel uncomfortable parked at the convenience store, just drive to one of the motels and park there for a while. I'd suggest checking into a room, but I don't think it will be necessary."

We followed the route Levko had shown me. Just past the Pines Guy's access drive, I had Karla stop at a wide spot on the shoulder. I got out and she turned the car around and disappeared back in the direction we'd come.

There wasn't any need for bushwhacking—the house was a good half mile in—so I walked up the access drive, not bothering to conceal myself until I was about a hundred yards from the house. From my approach, the ground sloped gradually down toward the house, giving me a good view of both the front and the open area to the left. Like the night with Levko, there were outside lights burning, but inside, the house was dark. I stopped behind a low thicket of manzanita to

205

consider the layout and to give a little thought to why I was doing this.

People often say they don't believe in coincidence, that there is no such thing as coincidence, that everything happens for a reason. Once someone is operating under this kind of misconception, it's only natural to take the extra step and put yourself at the center of the drama, where the reasons that drive the universe orbit around you. Even if you aren't vulnerable to this particular delusion, when something really improbable happens, it's natural to suspect some agency of operating behind the scenes. Sheer improbability makes us incredulous of chance. But the truth is, the world is so densely replete with possibilities that seemingly improbable juxtapositions are commonplace. Things bang into each other not because of any grand design, but just because there are so many things moving around. Patterns arise out of deeper patterns, linger briefly, then fade back into the vastness.

Still, sometimes something will happen, something so improbable it's difficult to resist the feeling that events have been staged for your benefit. Sometimes you can hardly believe your eyes. That was pretty much where I found myself, standing in the woods outside the Pines Guy's house: dumbfounded, having trouble believing my eyes.

The silence had suddenly been broken by the sound of the front door being flung open. A young girl, maybe in her late teens, stumbled out, confused. She spun one way, then the other, not sure where she was or which way to go, then ran across the open yard, fleeing whatever was inside the house. Two seconds later, a man stepped through the door, not hurrying, but nonetheless clearly interested in the fleeing girl. He took several steps away from the house, then stopped, his eyes moving up the slope to the thicket where I was concealed. Only I knew I wasn't concealed—not from the eyes that had fixed directly on me. I knew he could see me as clearly as I could see him, because the man standing in the yard was not a man. I had not seen those eyes for a hundred years. The Pines Guy was Calvin, the vampire who a century earlier had turned me.

The girl, as if determined to add to the improbable, did the same thing the two fighting cats had done a few nights before: she ran straight at me, blindly, scrambling through the underbrush, like a wild animal panicked by the chemistry of fear. When she came within reach, I grabbed her by the wrist. She screamed and started flailing, not so much as if she were trying to escape my grip, but as if she were suddenly possessed by an overwhelming and incomprehensible fury. As if after thinking she had escaped, the misfortune of being so quickly caught again was too much for her, and her mind snapped. I yanked her close and covered her mouth. I assume she continued to struggle, but at the moment I wasn't paying much attention. Calvin hadn't moved. We stared at each other for what must have been a full minute, then he did the same thing he'd done the first time our paths crossed. He turned around and walked calmly back into the house and closed the door.

The sound of the door closing was like an off-switch. There was a moment of culminating stillness, and then, as if the switch were flipped the other way, something became clear to me for the first time. A hundred years ago in Sicily, Calvin had turned his back and walked away. He did it knowing how vulnerable I was. He knew there was a good chance I'd make some stupid mistake and end up paying for it with my life. In the intervening hundred years, I had harbored a resentment at what I assumed was his callousness toward my fate. But now, standing there in the woods, I understood for the first time that the callousness, if in fact it had been callousness, was not what I resented. What I resented was being taken for granted.

"The thirst will educate you. Nothing else matters." That's what Calvin had said. At the time I had no idea what he was talking about. But as the years passed, his words continued to haunt and irritate me. I could neither forget them nor accept them. His blithe assumption that I could be reduced to the satisfaction of a thirst, that there was nothing in me that was not subservient to, and made insignificant by, my dietary requirements, still ate at me. And now, a hundred years later, wasn't he making the same assumption? Wasn't he assuming he could leave the girl in my hands because he could take it for granted that the thirst would settle everything? Wasn't he assuming that because we were both vampires, my choices would be the same as his choices; my choices would flow from blood because, as a vampire, I had been reduced to blood? That's what I resented: that I could be reduced to blood.

I don't know how much time had passed before I realized the girl was having trouble breathing. "Don't scream," I said, then took my hand off her mouth. She sucked air like she'd been too long under water. I could smell the blood where her bare feet had been scraped and cut during her escape. She was thin and unkempt and stank of fear.

It didn't make sense. Why would Calvin bother with bringing a girl back to his house? Was he holding people and siphoning their blood? Why would he complicate his life like that? I just couldn't see it. That kind of blood farming was way too risky and way too much work. It was far simpler, cleaner and more efficient to go hunting. By the same logic, there was a simple and clean answer to the question of what I should do with this girl. She was a free meal. I could simply drink her blood and walk away, leaving the corpse for Calvin to dispose of.

That was my initial inclination. The minutes passed. The girl had dropped to her knees, no longer squirming. My grip on her wrist was all that stopped her from collapsing completely. I wanted there to be people who deserved to be taken off the menu. Was this girl, mewing in limp defeat, one of them? And if so, what distinguished her? I really had no idea, and the dilemma was maddening.

"Don't scream," I said again, then draped the girl over my shoulder like a sack of bones and started back to the road.

I called Karla and she met us a few minutes later where she'd dropped me off. The girl had been whimpering softly most of the way, but seemed to settle down when I put her in the front seat of the car. Karla's jaw dropped when she saw the girl, but she didn't waste any time getting practical. She cranked up the car's heater, then took off her jacket and wrapped it around the girl's shoulders.

"She's fucking freezing, Shake! Give me your windbreaker."

I did as I was told and Karla wrapped it around the girl's feet. When she was satisfied with her ministrations, she asked, "Is this the missing girl?" apparently having jumped to the conclusion that I'd found the Arnauds' niece.

I shook my head no, which seemed to disappoint her.

"Who is she, Shake?"

"I don't know."

"What? You just found her in the woods?"

"Why don't we head back to Sacramento," I said, wanting to put some distance between us and Calvin.

Karla turned back to the girl. "Are you okay, honey?" she asked, making an adjustment to the windbreaker. The girl smiled weakly and nodded. Karla put the car in gear and headed back toward the freeway.

I was wondering if the girl knew where she was, if she would be able to lead someone back to Calvin's house. I leaned forward so I could see her. She was a lot smaller than Karla. Wrapped in the oversized jacket, she looked like a child. Her eyes were open but unfocused. "What's your name?" I asked.

She blinked but didn't look up at me when she spoke. "Joy."

"Do you know where you are, Joy?"

Again, without raising her eyes, "No sir."

I hadn't caught it when she'd said her name, but there was enough accent in the "no sir" to place her from the south. "Where are you from, Joy?"

"Galveston, Texas."

"How long have you been at that house?"

She finally raised her eyes and looked at me when she answered. "Two weeks maybe. I'm not sure. He was taking my blood."

That got Karla's attention. "What's she talking about, Shake?" Then to the girl, "Who was taking your blood?"

I knew I was going to have to do some explaining to Karla, but I preferred not to do it in front of the girl. "Is that where you were, in Galveston, before someone brought you here?"

"Yes sir. I mean, no sir. I live in Galveston, but I was visiting San Francisco."

"You have family in Texas?"

"Yes sir."

"Do you want to go back?" I asked.

"Yes sir," she said, starting to cry, "I do."

We rode in silence as far as Folsom where I had Karla exit the freeway and we found an all-night Rite Aid. The girl had fallen asleep and didn't wake up until the car stopped. Yawning, she raised herself enough to look out the window. Apparently satisfied that she didn't have the slightest idea where she was or why, she settled back down in the seat, curling up under Karla's jacket.

While Karla was in the store, I puzzled over what to do with Joy. The airport wouldn't work. Without ID, she wouldn't be able to buy a ticket and security wouldn't let her board a plane. I called Amtrak on my cell phone. There was only one train per day going south, and it had already passed through Sacramento. That meant she'd have to take the bus.

Karla came back with two bottles of water, paper towels, disinfectant, socks, a pair of cheap tennis shoes, two sweatshirts, and a couple of energy bars. I had Joy move to the back seat with me, and told Karla to take us to the L Street Greyhound depot in Sacramento. While the girl ate the two energy bars and finished off one of the bottles of water, I used the other bottle to clean and disinfect the cuts on her feet.

I suggested she get rid of the t-shirt she was wearing. She looked down at the dirt and stains, then pulled it off without modesty. She was thin as a rail. She looked at her arms, rubbing her fingers lightly over the bruised needle marks at both elbows.

211

"He was taking my blood," she said again, as if she wanted to be sure I understood.

I pointed to the two sweatshirts. She selected one and pulled it on, thought about it for a second, then pulled the second one on over the first. Karla hadn't asked the girl her shoe size, but the tennis shoes looked just right. A good example, I thought, of how naturally attentive Karla was to the details of her surroundings. If she wasn't a vampire's chauffeur, she would have made a good CIA operative.

Just to settle the matter of the Arnauds' niece, there was something I wanted to ask the girl before we got to the bus depot. "Joy, were there other girls at that house with you?"

"There was another girl," she said quietly.

"Do you know her name?"

"I never talked to her. I only heard her."

She seemed to be embarrassed about something.

"That's how I got away," she continued. "The other girl started screaming, and the man left my door unlocked when he went to see why."

"So you never saw her?"

"I saw her once. Just for a second."

"What did she look like?"

"I think she was Chinese, or something. Just a little kid."

"No one else?" I asked.

"No sir, I don't think so."

When we got to the Greyhound station, I waited in the car while Karla took Joy inside. She was gone for about half an hour. When she came back, she got in the car without saying anything, and sat for several minutes, fidgeting with the keys while she thought about what she wanted to say.

"The bus doesn't leave until 8:15," she said, finally.

"Do you think she'll get on it?" I asked.

"I guess so." Then added, as if she wasn't sure how I would react, "I gave her some money."

"That was thoughtful."

"I gave her a thousand dollars," she clarified.

"It's expense money. For you to use at your discretion."

She put the key in the ignition, but didn't start the car. "Shake, I know I'm not supposed to ask a lot questions, but it would really help me if you told me what happened to that girl."

She was almost pleading. "Help you?" I asked.

"Yes. Help me make sense out of what's going on. Who was she?"

"You know as much about her as I do. She's just a young girl who got caught in something, through no fault of her own, and then she got lucky."

"So you won't tell me?" she said, looking me in the eye so I'd know how unacceptable that was to her.

"To be honest, Karla, there are things I can't explain, and telling you part of the story won't put your mind at ease."

"Jesus, Shake! We just rescued that girl from some psycho-fuck kidnapper, and instead of taking her to the cops, we put her on a bus to fucking Texas. And that's supposed to be the end of it? Like, I'm not supposed to be curious?"

"Look, Karla. I know I'm asking a lot of you, but we've done everything we can. The girl was in trouble and we helped her. That should be enough."

Karla folded her arms tightly across her chest, clearly disinclined to let it go. "What about that asshole in the mountains. Joy said he has another girl. What about her?"

213

And now, I thought, for the hard part. "I can't do anything about that, Karla."

"Can't or won't?" she asked, again staring me in the face.

"Both, I'm afraid."

"I don't get it," she said, exasperated. "Who the fuck is this guy? Are you, like, afraid of him, or something?"

"I'm not exactly afraid of him."

Karla studied my face, her mood shifting from frustration to one of curious surprise. "You know him, don't you?"

"Our paths crossed once, a long time ago."

"Jesus, Shake!"

"I'm not afraid of what he might do to me, Karla. I don't think he's a threat to me, any more than I'm a threat to him. But I don't really know him. If I interfere, he might get vindictive. He might come after you, and I don't want that. And believe me, you don't, either."

"We could tell the police. We could report him, like, anonymously, or something."

"You can't imagine how pointless that would be."

"What about Mio? She could help us."

Bringing up Mio took me completely by surprise.

"She could help us," Karla said, more optimistically, "couldn't she?"

"Maybe she could," I granted, "but I don't think she would. Either way, I can't ask her for help. Not with this. And I can't explain why. You just have to accept that Mio is not an option."

Sensing the finality in my voice, Karla tried one last tack. "What if I reported him on my own?"

"It sounds like you're asking me what I'll do if you report

him against my advice not to."

Karla looked at me but didn't say anything.

"You're free to do as you wish, Karla. I can understand you wanting to help the other girl. But going to the police won't do her any good."

"You can't be sure of that."

"As I said, the choice is yours."

"You really won't do anything?"

"I'll give you some good advice. Don't go anywhere near that house in Pollock Pines, ever again. It's not in your power to hurt the man who lives there. Neither you nor the police are going to do anything other than inconvenience him. As for the girl, my guess is she's already gone. He won't take any chances after Joy got away from him. The last thing you want to do is give him a reason to notice your existence, a reason to single you out."

"Is he really that dangerous?"

"He's dangerous in ways you can't imagine. And he's playing by a very different set of rules. That might not sound important to you, but it is. He's willing to do things your humanity won't allow, things you wouldn't dream of doing. And that makes him unpredictable and extremely dangerous."

We were nearing the university. Karla hadn't said anything for several blocks. As we approached the footbridge, I told Karla to turn around, giving her directions to American River Drive.

"You can drop me off at my house," I said.

"Wow! The mysterious Shake is going to show me where he lives."

"I understand why you're upset. I understand that the

injustice of this is difficult to ignore. But this is one of those times when you need to step back and pause."

Karla gripped the steering wheel with both hands and took several long, deep breaths. "Let me see if I've got this straight. You want me to trust you about not reporting a psycho who kidnaps and probably tortures and murders young girls, and in return you're going to trust me with your address!"

"Have you read Borges?" I asked.

The question clearly confused her. "What?" she asked, shaking her head as if to clear it.

"The writer, Jorge Luis Borges."

"I've heard of him," she said.

"In one of his fictions, a character searches through the pockets of a dead man and finds a small metal cone that is so heavy, he can barely lift it. The man is mystified by this inexplicable object and, of course, he steals it. Unfortunately for him, the cone has a deleterious effect on anyone in possession of it, and the man comes, as they say, to a bad end."

"And your point is?" she said, after I'd paused.

"My point is that having my address may not be as light a matter as you think."

I had her pull up in front of the house. "This is it," I said. "I live on the second floor. The caretaker lives downstairs. There's a private entrance in the back."

We sat quietly for a bit, Karla's face turned away from me as she studied the house.

"It's a nice house," she said, breaking the silence. "I guess I'm a little surprised."

"Why is that?"

"I don't know. It's just an ordinary house on an ordinary

street. I guess I was expecting something more mysterious."

I could see she was calming down. We sat a while longer in silence before she spoke again.

"I'll do what you want, Shake. I'll stay away from Pollock Pines. And I won't call the police." Then, after a minute of silence, asked, "Will you do me a favor?"

"Certainly, if I can."

"When Mio is back in town, would you tell her I'd like to go dancing again?"

"I'm sure she'll be pleased," I said, and got out.

22

The garage was separated from the house by a passageway giving access to the back yard. As I passed through the gate, I knew I had company and I knew who it was. When I rounded the corner into the back yard, Calvin was on the upstairs landing, leaning against the banister. He seemed to be preoccupied with his thoughts, remaining motionless as I started up the stairs. Only as I neared the top did he turn and face me. He had changed very little in the hundred years since we had last stood so close. His eyes were still cold, piercing, indifferent; the gaze of a well-fed predator. Or maybe it was just the gaze of someone who had seen most of what there was to see in this world. In Sicily, he had been dressed like one of the local shopkeepers. Now he was wearing khaki slacks with oversized pockets on the thighs, hiking boots, and a wrinkled cotton shirt.

"You let the girl go," he said, with the hint of a smile. It wasn't a question so much as a request to confirm what he assumed to be the case.

"Yes," I said.

Having gotten confirmation, he seemed to be considering his next words, then added, with the low, whispery tranquility I remembered first hearing under the rubble in Sicily, "It will be inconvenient for me, if she leads the police back to my house."

"I don't think that will happen. She has no idea where she was, and I put her on a bus to Texas."

There was an unexpected sparkle in his eyes. "You're either more heartless than I am, or you've never been to Texas."

His comment was funny, but I wasn't in the mood. "It seemed like the thing to do under the circumstances."

"Circumstances?" he asked.

That was when it suddenly became clear to me. I'd done the same thing to Calvin as he had done to me. I had taken him for granted. For a hundred years, I had satisfied myself with an idea of him that was mostly my own invention, one that I'd formed while still under the sway of my human emotions. My first impressions hadn't been entirely wrong. Calvin was indifferent to my fate, but no more so than I was to his. What I couldn't see in Sicily was the practicality behind his lack of emotional involvement. I couldn't understand his detachment from the devastation all around him, because at the time I lacked that detachment myself. But a century had now passed.

Be that as it may, I still wasn't inclined to explain myself to him. I wasn't particularly uncomfortable about finding him at my house. I didn't care that he knew where I lived. I wasn't afraid of him. But something was changing for me, something I wasn't very clear about in my own mind, and Calvin, what he represented, was from a past I was trying to move away from, or at least trying to reevaluate. But then it occurred to me that if I wanted to take a fresh look at my past, Calvin might be the best place to start.

"You're not still upset about Sicily, are you?" he asked. Then, when I didn't respond, he said, "Look, I know what happened there was hard for you. I admit I might have been more helpful."

"You think?"

"You say that like it's obvious I could have made things easier for you. But it isn't. It's far from obvious. Being turned can be positively chaotic. I wasn't in any better position to predict what you would do, how well or poorly you would handle the situation, than you were."

I had to admit, Calvin had a point. There was no way he could have known what I might do those first few weeks. "It doesn't matter anymore," I said. "But I am curious. Why did you walk away like that?"

Calvin raised his right hand, as if examining something resting in his palm. "I had no intention of turning you that night. If not for the earthquake, you would have died along with your wife. But once it was done, I had no real choice but to accept it. However, that didn't make me responsible for you. I'm not your daddy. I had no more obligation to you then than you have to me now. As it was, my situation in Messina was getting precarious. I didn't want you blundering along behind me. As things turned out, I left the island shortly after the quake."

I knew well enough from my own experience how precarious the situation with humans could become. "I can accept that. We agree, then, that I have no obligation to you?"

"None that makes any sense to me."

"Then why come here asking questions?"

For the first time, his gaze seemed to soften slightly. "Are you always this inhospitable?" he asked.

Again, I realized I was acting like I had a grudge against him. "Not always," I said, trying to be more accommodating.

Calvin scanned the night sky. "It's going to be light soon. If you don't invite me inside, I'll have to be on my way."

There wasn't any reason not to invite him in, and I was curious about why he was there, so I unlocked the door and ushered him in.

"Nice place," Calvin said, looking around before making himself comfortable on the sofa. "How's this working out for you?"

"It works well enough."

"Do those curtains keep out the sunlight?"

"Most of it, and the window glass is polarized."

"And the guy downstairs is a friend of Mio's, I take it?"

"If that was a question, it sounds like you already know the answer."

"Just a guess. I'm also guessing Mio never mentioned to you that we've met?"

"No, she didn't," I admitted.

"Just once. About two years ago. I was up at Lake Tahoe. I saw her get out of a limo and go into one of the casinos. I knew immediately she was one of us. Humans don't move like that. And I was pretty sure who she was. After all, there aren't many Japanese vampires her size who dress like royalty and ride around in a limousine. So I followed her into the casino."

"You talked to her?" I asked.

"She was waiting for me. That surprised me. Apparently she'd noticed me watching her when she arrived. I don't mean to brag, but I'm pretty good at not being noticed."

"What did you talk about?"

"Not much, really. She wasn't exactly friendly when I told her who I was. I suspect that if we hadn't been in the casino she would have practiced her kung fu on me."

"Why would she do that?"

"To tell you the truth, I think it had something to do with you. I think she was warning me."

Calvin seemed to be waiting for a response, but there

wasn't much to say. If he was right, I was pleased to know that Mio had my interests at heart. But I wasn't going to tell Calvin that.

"Do the two of you get together often?" he asked.

"Only when she's in town. Why?"

"I suppose I'm impressed. We only spoke for a few minutes, but Mio strikes me as capable of being either graciously accommodating or viciously unpleasant, depending on her own private whims."

"That impresses you?"

"What impresses me is how different the two of you are, and yet you seem to have a durable relationship. One that evidently works for both of you. That isn't easy to come by. You and I are a lot alike in that regard. We both find most of our fellow vampires disappointing. Wouldn't you agree?"

"'Disappointing' is a generous way to put it."

"Yes," he said, as if distracted again examining his empty hand. "I suppose it is."

"You were going to tell me why you're here."

"For one thing, as I already mentioned, I was concerned that your good deed with the girl might have put my living arrangements in jeopardy."

"I'm sorry," I said, meaning it.

"Would you mind telling me what you were doing in Pollock Pines?"

"I was looking for someone. A girl, but not the one that ran out of your house."

"So, you didn't know I lived there?"

"The possibility had never crossed my mind."

"You must have been surprised. I certainly was, when I

saw you in the woods. I knew you lived here in Sacramento, but I never expected to see you up there in the mountains."

Calvin seemed to know a lot more about me than I knew about him.

"So, why were you looking for this other girl?" he asked, as if there were no conceivable reason why I wouldn't tell him.

"It's complicated. Let's just say I'd started something and I wanted to finish it."

"And it was this something you wanted to finish, trying to find this other girl, that led you to my door."

"Yes."

"Did the path to Pollock Pines lead through Yavorsky?" he asked.

"Not directly. One of Yavorsky's employees. A guy named Levko. The one who delivered the girls to your house."

Calvin was thoughtful for a minute before speaking again. "I'm sure you can appreciate my concern, Shake. Yavorsky has his uses, but he's not very bright and that makes him unreliable. If any of this is going to be a problem for me, I'd like to know before it gets out of hand."

"I don't think you have anything to worry about from Levko. All he did was show me your house. I've never laid eyes on Yavorsky and he doesn't know who I am or that Levko met with me. Levko seems to be genuinely afraid of him. Or at any rate, afraid for his family back in Ukraine."

"He should be. Yavorsky is a real piece of work."

"Levko seems to have a similar opinion of you."

"Yes, well, he knew where to deliver the girls. I wanted it to be clear to him that that was all he needed to know."

"About that... having people delivered like pizzas. Why

would you do that?"

"I realize it must seem a little foolish. Kidnapping humans is so much more complicated than killing them, as I suspect you may have figured out for yourself over the years. Unfortunately, keeping them on hand was necessary at times."

"And you used someone like Yavorsky to get them?"

"Who else would I use? People who market in young girls aren't driven by ethical principles. It was risky, I admit. I did my own procuring, as much as I could. That's what I was doing in Tahoe when I ran into Mio, looking for a body to snatch."

We both seemed to be dancing around the obvious question. "Why would you need to keep them on hand?"

"I needed their blood for something other than drinking."

"You didn't drink their blood?" I asked, genuinely curious where this was headed.

"Well, I drank a little, on occasion. A sip now and then. But I needed it for something else. Which brings me to the other reason for paying you a visit." Calvin stretched his legs and settled himself more comfortably into the sofa cushions. "A while back, in the early part of the twentieth century, I started looking into the possibility of a cure for our intolerance to sunlight. Initially, my efforts were rather farcical, as you might imagine. Given the state of medical science at the time, not to mention my own complete ignorance of biochemistry, the chances of success weren't very good. I'm sure you'd get a kick out of some of the harebrained concoctions I came up with. You've probably seen some of those old film clips of man's early attempts to build flying machines—you know, men jumping off cliffs with goofy mechanical bird wings strapped to their arms, that sort of thing. My early efforts were more or less comparable.

The only reason I survived my experiments was because my vampire metabolism was impregnable to my own half-baked determination to poison myself.

"I'd pretty much given up after a few decades of using myself as a lab rat. Then, in the fifties, Crick and Watson discovered the double helix structure of DNA and I began to think maybe a cure wasn't so far-fetched. I spent a few years getting myself up to speed in the related sciences. But as the decades passed, the more I learned, the more difficult it became to pursue research in the directions that seemed the most promising."

"Facilities?"

"Among other things. There is a serious technology barrier. The tools get harder and harder to procure. The laboratories are in a constant state of technological evolution. Much of the research consists of inventing and developing the research tools, themselves. Everything tends to be shrouded behind patents. And even if you have access to the equipment, it's so expensive, you need a mountain of venture capital to afford it."

"I can see where being a vampire might not encourage investors," I said.

"Indeed. But being a vampire isn't the real problem. Seventy or eighty years ago, my research consisted mainly of concocting ingestible or injectable chemical compounds. My efforts may have been poorly understood and misguided, but they weren't incommensurate with the scientific procedures of their day. But as biology progressed deeper and deeper into molecular-level mysteries, and as the various specialized disciplines branched and multiplied, it became more and more difficult for me to keep pace. My so-called research inevitably grew more and more fanciful. Eventually I had to accept the fact that I was a dilettante, at best, dabbling in something that was way beyond me."

"But you've continued to dabble?"

"Yes, but that's all it is. All it has been for quite a few years, now. Just a hobby."

"So the people you were keeping at your house," I asked, for some reason wanting to have it spelled out. "Their blood was for your hobby?"

Calvin only looked at me, as if the answer to my question was obvious enough not to require an actual response.

"And you haven't made any progress?" I asked.

"Nothing substantial, I'm afraid. A few ideas that might be worth looking into. But I've gone as far as I can on my resources."

"But you think a cure is still worth pursuing?"

"I really don't know. I'm not convinced it isn't."

Calvin leaned his head back against the sofa cushion and closed his eyes. I was thinking about what he'd told me when it dawned on me why he was there. "Mio's financial resources," I said.

Calvin smiled and then opened his eyes. "Mio is preposterously wealthy, plus she owns a controlling interest in several companies that are already invested in biological and genetic research. She could easily incorporate my work into existing programs."

"I don't get it. Why not talk to Mio yourself?"

"I would have when we met at Tahoe. But she was too busy making sure I wasn't going to bother you. So I dropped it.

Then you showed up at my house in Pollock Pines and... well, put a bug in the program."

Calvin said this as if the consequences of what had happened were of no real concern to him, but the girl's escape had clearly been a potential problem.

"The truth is," he continued, "I'm not worried about it. In fact, I'm half glad things turned out this way. I've been putting something off, something that requires my attention elsewhere. Your visit was just the little nudge I needed." As Calvin said this, he took a CD jewel case out of his shirt pocket. "I'd like you to give this to Mio," he said, laying it on the sofa cushion. "As I said, I've pretty much hit the limit of what I can accomplish on my own. The DVD is all my notes, everything that might possibly be useful, should Mio be interested in continuing my research."

Calvin leaned back and closed his eyes again. The dissonance between the idea of Calvin that I had retained for so long, and the thoughtfully calm, half-whispered modulations of his voice was slightly unnerving. I looked at the disc in its jewel case, wondering how many hours of work, over how many decades, were encoded on that piece of plastic.

"If she is interested, do you want her to get in touch with you?"

"Not really. I'd prefer to be done with it," he said, not opening his eyes.

"What if she finds a cure?"

"If that happens, I'll hear about it, sooner or later."

The contents of the disc represented years of work looking for something that had finally eluded Calvin. By giving the disc to Mio, was he hoping to salvage something? Or could he simply open his hand and let go of a piece of himself, like dropping a book that no longer held his interest? His reasons for visiting may have been more complicated than he was letting on, but they may not have been. Either way, I found myself feeling there was something admirable in his actions; something larger in spirit than I had granted him a century ago in Sicily.

"I'll give her the disc," I said.

"Thank you. I'm glad that's settled."

"There's something you might be able to settle for me, if you don't mind."

Calvin opened his eyes and waited.

"Miriam Moore," I said.

Several seconds passed before his expression betrayed a hint of recognition. "The girl you were looking for?"

"Yes."

"She was one of Yavorsky's."

"She's dead, then?" I asked.

"About a year ago. What was she to you?"

"Just a piece in a puzzle. I didn't know her."

Calvin seemed to consider my words. "Is this something you often do?" he asked.

"Is what something I often do?"

"Meddle in the affairs of people?"

"When it serves my purposes. You do the same."

"I know it's none of my business. I'm just curious about how you get along in the world. From the looks of things—this house, for example, your relationship with Mio—you seem to be able to cope well enough. I'm impressed, to tell the truth. Very few vampires can pull it off."

"You seem to do all right," I said.

Calvin stood up and began pacing around the room. Several times he seemed about to say something, then changed his mind and continued pacing. This went on for a good ten minutes before he finally spoke again.

"Let me ask you a question, Shake. Why is it that you don't associate with other vampires? And before you answer, let me say that we're very similar in this regard. I may be even more reclusive than you are."

The question wasn't difficult. "I simply don't like them," I said. "The ones I've met, anyway. Their idiosyncrasies are too exaggerated. They're repulsive as individuals and even worse in groups."

Calvin nodded. "I feel pretty much the same way. I've often asked myself why congeniality or simple cooperation is so rare among us. There are exceptions, of course. You and Mio, for example. But the exceptions are just that. Exceptional. On the face of it, you wouldn't think it would be any more difficult for vampires to get along than it is for people. But the fact is, we don't."

For a long time, I'd thought of my distaste for other vampires as an aspect of my own personality. It had only been in the last few decades that I'd begun to see it as a problem characteristic of vampires in general. "I've wondered about that myself," I said. "Why vampires seem to be so relentlessly disobliging toward one another."

"Relentlessly disobliging," Calvin repeated. Then added, somehow managing to look sheepish, "In other words, they're all rather like you, wouldn't you say?"

"I suppose so."

"Why do you think that is?"

I thought about the question, but didn't see any obvious answer.

"I'll tell you what I think," Calvin said. "We have a problem with power. I know I'm generalizing. But the fact is, vampires will almost always prefer to wield their own power rather than sublimate their desires to some group purpose. We all want to be on top, which ultimately means that we can't trust or rely on one another."

"Humans are pretty much the same," I said.

"Yes, but there's a crucial difference. There are billions of people on the planet. Most of them lack the power to dominate their own children, much less other adults. But because people are so numerous, the weaker ones can form alliances that give them powers they lack as individuals. These alliances have evolved into very complex networks of social and cultural forces that allow people to thrive in the absence of any real physical or psychological or intellectual efficacy. This is very straightforward for most people. They see that they are better off playing by some set of rules, no matter how arbitrary. They know they can't buck the system, and they know they can't take charge. So they do the smart thing and cooperate. They trade their independence for security and social status and all the other complex social rewards. They gather into groups to compensate for an underlying weakness that vampires don't share. For us, it's more natural to shun cooperation. We prefer to rely on ourselves. And that, as I suspect you understand very well, puts us in a tenuous position."

"You mean in our relationships with people?" I asked.

"Exactly. We need human beings for more than their blood. We need them as a mirror. A vampire can't survive in absolute solitude. Without a mirror, we lose self-awareness, and without self-awareness, we regress to an animal state."

"Where life is nasty, brutish and short, as Hobbes so succinctly put it."

"Except in our case, it would be nasty, brutish and long."

And there I was, back to the same question: Who to kill? If all I needed from people was a supply of blood, it wouldn't make any difference who I took it from. But if I needed people for more than that, if I needed people in order to see who and what I was, then it was in my best interest to spare the lives of people who were, in some way, better mirrors. Unfortunately, even if this made sense—and I wasn't sure it did—I still didn't know what made some people better mirrors than others. Which meant I still lacked the same thing I'd always lacked: a way to choose. It wasn't any easier to identify a good mirror than it was to identify a good person. And thinking about it in this way was probably just an invitation to confuse the good with the flattering.

Still, there had to be people who, as mirrors, were better able to reflect things of value. And if there were such people, then what could make them better mirrors if not the fact that they were somehow better people? Clearly, there were people I could kill without undermining my own awareness. People like Danny Weiss, for instance. Or Bill, the psycho who had terrorized Karla that night in Sloughhouse. And if there were negatives, then there had to be positives. There had to be people who reflected a better picture of the world.

"When you think about it," Calvin said, interrupting my thoughts, "it really isn't all that mysterious. We, you and I, don't like the company of other vampires because they reflect too much of what is ugly and aberrant in us. Fortunately, we can get by without them. We don't like the company of most people because, lacking any real strength of character, they reflect too much of what is weak and inadequate in us. Unfortunately, we can't get by without them."

"How do you choose?" I asked, the question popping out on its own.

"How do I choose what?" he asked.

"Whose blood to take?"

Calvin stood up and quietly paced the room for several minutes. "If I correctly understand the motivation behind your question, what you want to ask is: How do I decide whose blood not to take?"

"Yes," I agreed, "that's the question."

Calvin paced some more before answering. "What should I do? A question people have been asking for thousands of years, and they've come up with quite an array of answers, everything from the carefully reasoned arguments of philosophers, to the tritest clichés of the simpleminded, to the preposterous ravings of lunatics. In the end, it's difficult to say if the philosophers have gotten any closer than the lunatics. But one thing seems certain to me. The search itself is perilous for the simple reason that it's so easy and so tempting to convince yourself you've found an answer, when in fact you haven't. Don't get me wrong. It's better to search than not to search. It's just that, in retrospect, it often seems like it would have been better not to search, rather than delude yourself about what you've found."

"Does that mean you've stopped asking?"

"In a way, yes. I was turned in 1581. You can do the math. That's a lot of time to be wrong in, and I have to admit, I haven't wasted the opportunity."

I had no idea Calvin was that old. "So it has been a problem for you, deciding who not to kill?" I asked.

"Of course it's a problem. The problem of value: Why is one life worth more than another? I've never come up with an answer that would hold water. But it's not as much of a problem for me as it used to be."

"Because you stopped asking?"

"No, because now I think there are mysteries that are better left as mysteries. There are questions I'm never going to be able to answer, and I prefer not to delude myself into thinking that I have, or that I ever will."

I understood what Calvin was saying and my own experience suggested he was right. The difference between us seemed to be that Calvin had found a way to live without the answers, whereas I hadn't, not with any peace of mind.

"It's different for vampires than it is for people," Calvin continued. "You might say that humans have perfected the art of extracting benefit from falsehoods. If you want a good example of this, look at the Roman Catholic Church, or any other religion, for that matter. But for a vampire, there isn't much profit in the cultivation of falsehoods, because a vampire isn't part of the social structure those falsehoods buttress. We don't have to situate ourselves inside a social hierarchy in order to secure a better life for ourselves. We're not part of the fabric of the institutions—religion, politics, etc.—that exist primarily to give humans a way to gain status and power. This kind of willful delusion doesn't help a vampire get by. Or, at any rate, not vampires like you and me. Mio is arguably an exception. But for us, human society doesn't help much because its foundations are

233

built on greed, ignorance and fear. At bottom, people's rationales are all hopelessly incoherent. Vampires like you and me are better off staying away from all of that."

"It sounds to me like what you're saying is that it's a mistake for a vampire to ask questions that are fundamentally human."

"I don't mean to go that far. The questions aren't the problem. But there are a lot traps along the road to answering them. People fall into those traps by sabotaging their own critical faculties. Human beings have to anesthetize themselves against the inadequacy of their answers. A vampire shouldn't have to do that."

I was intrigued by what Calvin had said, but it didn't help me resolve the problem of who not to kill. "I don't see a practical solution in any of this," I said. "How does this help you choose?"

"A hundred years ago," Calvin said, "I walked away and left you to fend for yourself. I wasn't happy about it, but as I've already explained, there were reasons for what I did. I can't change the past. I don't even want to. Our respective situations are much different now, and the truth is, Shake, I rather like you. I'm surprised by that. I would like to give you an answer, but I'm not sure I have one that would be of any use to you."

"Useful or not, you could just answer the question."

For several minutes, Calvin examined the palms of his hands, as if he couldn't quite believe how empty they were. "This isn't advice," he said. "It's just how things look to me."

I didn't see any reason to say anything, so I didn't.

"If I ask myself whether someone in particular deserves to live, the only way I can decide is by short-circuiting the question.

234

I don't really know what qualities go into exempting a human being from my nutritional needs. I can't walk through a crowd of people and pick out the ones who merit exemption. Whatever it is that makes someone distinctively valuable, it isn't obvious to an observer. At least, not to this observer. In order to choose, I have to resort to something too arbitrary and too vague to articulate: a feeling, an intuition, a sense of something that, ultimately, I don't understand. If I do that, I know I'm simply falling back on built-in prejudices that tip the scales one way or the other, for reasons that elude me. I suspect you know exactly what I mean."

"I think I do," I said.

"This wouldn't be a problem, except that I, like you, want to know why the scales tip one way rather than the other. But since I've never been able to answer that question in any satisfactory way, I ask a different question. I ask who deserves to die."

I couldn't see how that question would be any easier to answer, and said as much.

"What makes the second question answerable is that I'm intimately familiar with evil. I may not know what good is, but I can look into myself and see its opposite. All the coldness, the savagery, the ruthless, calculating indifference, are as familiar to me as the palms of my hands. But what makes the question answerable is that there are human beings just like me. And the strange thing is, those people also know when they see evil, because they are also intimately familiar with it. When they see me, when we make eye contact, I'm like a mirror in which they catch a glimpse of themselves. When that happens, and it happens more often than you might think, there is a moment of recognition that is unmistakable. When I see that spark of recognition, I know I've found my next meal."

Under different circumstances, I would have thought Calvin was, as they say, fucking with me. The idea that he could see evil acknowledge itself struck me as pretty far-fetched, and my doubt must have been apparent to Calvin.

"Like I said, it's not advice. I'm just telling you what works for me."

"So you only kill these so-called evil people?" I asked.

"Not only, but mostly. I think of it as my way of balancing accounts. I realize the accounts are imaginary. Just a story I tell myself. There is no cosmic balance sheet. But it's a story that seems amenable to my predilections, and it's the best I can do."

"I can see you're serious," I said, not sure what else to say.

"I suppose there's a certain twisted logic to it. Evil defeated by greater evil in the name of something good. But the logic is definitely of the twisted variety."

"I wasn't expecting you to be impressed," Calvin said. "But if you think about it, I think you'll see it's not so crazy. Look at yourself. Human culture offers you a lot of ease and enjoyment. This comfortable suburban house you live in, the music and literature and all the other arts you enjoy, the conveniences of modern technology. All of this is above the contribution people make to your nutritional health and, ultimately, to your sanity. I benefit from all these things the same as you do. As a rule, the people I kill aren't instrumental in creating this culture. They're like me. They don't contribute. They just take, and in the process, they take it for granted that the world is there for them to exploit as they please. They are, in a word, bloodsuckers. Reducing their numbers is my contribution."

•

The conversation trailed off after that. I think we were both talked out. We chatted a while longer, waiting for the sun to set. Calvin told me some interesting and amusing anecdotes about other vampires he'd known over the centuries. I entertained him in turn with some funny stories of my own.

When the sun was all the way down, Calvin got up from the sofa, stretched, and said it was time to go. I opened the door and we walked out onto the balcony. The sky was overcast and a chill wind rustled the leaves of the trees.

"I enjoyed our conversation," Calvin said, though the tone of his voice remained neutral. He offered his hand, which surprised me a little. I expected the shake to be perfunctory, in keeping, I suppose, with his emotional detachment. But he surprised me again by the firmness of his grip, stepping closer and gazing into my eyes. In that instant, there was a flicker of recognition in the depths of his gaze. For the briefest moment, his eyes were like a mirror in which I could see only myself.

23

"Hello, Shake," Karla said, when she answered the phone.

"Hello, Karla."

"What's up?"

"A couple of things. I want you to run an errand for me. I need you to drive down to San Francisco again, to Satellite. I want you to deliver a message for me. I don't care when you go. Any night in the next week or two is fine, except Mondays or Tuesdays. The guy I want you to see is off on those days."

"Hang on a second, Shake. Let me get a pencil. OK, go ahead."

"Go to Satellite and ask to speak to Levko."

"How do you spell that?"

"Like it sounds. L-E-V-K-O. Tell him you have a message from Shake. Tell him to call and leave a message at 916-101-2001 the next time Beketov is in town. B-E-K-E-T-O-V."

"That's it?"

"That's it. He's not going to like it, but tell him not to worry, just call and leave the message."

"And the other thing?"

"Pick me up at my house tomorrow night at 1:00 a.m. We're going to take another drive out to the Garden Highway."

The other thing was Ron Richardson.

Other books by Mel Nicolai:

The Case
7 Remote Mysteries & 1 Delay

Visit the author's website at
http://recklesspublications.com